BOOKER

WILKERSON DYNASTY BOOK 4

KATHI S. BARTON

This is a work of fiction. Names, characters, places, and incidents are products of the author's imagination or are used fictitiously and are not to be construed as real. Any resemblance to actual events, locations, organizations, or persons, living or dead, is entirely coincidental.

World Castle Publishing, LLC
Pensacola, Florida
Copyright © Kathi S. Barton 2021
Paperback ISBN: 9781956788242
eBook ISBN: 9781956788259
First Edition World Castle Publishing, LLC, November 8, 2021
http://www.worldcastlepublishing.com
Cover: Karen Fuller
Editor: Maxine Bringenberg

Prologue

Charlie wasn't sure what the hell she was doing. Not just here, but what she was to do if she wanted to bid on something. Abby and Amy had talked her and Rayne into coming up to this auction today to fill out their homes. She thought they had nice homes, but what did she know about being wealthy? Not a single thing.

The man she'd been sort of following was helping another man in things that he should bid on and how much. She had also learned not to take the first amount that the auctioneer put out there. It was only a starting point.

"Hello." She looked around when the man she was following spoke to her. "You haven't any idea what you're doing, do you?"

"Nope. I will admit I'm in well over my head. Like I need all kinds of things for this house I'm going to live in, but I haven't any idea how to go about it. Like, this table here. I love it. But I don't know what would be a good price to bid or how to even make that happen." He asked her if she had a number yet. "Yes. I got that when we first arrived. Abby told me about that."

"Abby? You're here with Abby Wilkerson?" She nodded, and the man laughed. "Well, isn't this a small world. I'm her cousin-in-law, Booker Wilkerson. I'm here with my cousin, Brandon."

"Will you help me?" He said he'd love to. "Good. First thing, this table. What is a good price to pay? I don't want to get caught up in the bidding and forget that I'm on a budget, somewhat."

"It's not old if that's what you're thinking." She asked him how he could tell that. "Look around at all the other pieces out here. What is the one thing they have in common? I know you can see it, but it never occurred to you yet."

She knew he wasn't talking about the age of the piece. To her, they all looked like they'd been around a long time. Then she noticed a few things she'd not before. Looking at Booker, she smiled.

"Someone has taken the time to dust this piece. Why would they do something like that to a piece that's just a table?" He told her. "I guess I can see that.

Polish it up so that it's more appealing to someone. Eye catching, I guess you could call it. So it will more than likely go a little high when it's probably just a table that isn't going to last all that long. Thank you."

"You're so very welcome. Also, you should never, if you can help it, linger too long when looking at a piece. That gives away that you're interested. Sort of casually look at something, then look around while keeping an eye on other people that look at it. You can figure out your competition that way." She giggled. Charlie told him he was wonderful for helping her. "I'm enjoying myself too, so it's good for us both."

They walked around together for the next half hour. Booker pointed out things she could bid on and how much she should go. He told her when she asked him if he'd help her when the bidding started that he'd love to, but he also had to help Brandon.

"Oh, I'm sorry. You did tell me you were here with him. You have given me a lot to go on, and I appreciate that." He told her he wasn't going to leave her. "But what about Brandon? Won't he be upset?"

"Right now, I don't care. You're much prettier than he is. Plus, he's hanging out with Abby. Who is, I might say, good at this too." The announcement was made that bidding would begin in five minutes. "Something else you might want to do when you go to an auction is to find out who the auctioneer is and make a mental note to watch how he does things. I ask where he might be starting when he begins and also if he will have a second auctioneer selling in another area. There is only the one person here until noon. Then they're going to sell the house and land around it. But he's going to start with the box lots. Those are the boxes of stuff that they deemed not worth too much, and they're getting rid of it. I find a lot of good things in those sort of boxes."

"Like what?" They were headed to the box-lots area now. "Oh, I understand now. They're literally boxes of just stuff. I think getting a couple of those would be a blast just to go through and see what junk you can find." She laughed.

"You'd be amazed at the things my Aunt Holly and I found in them." She was enjoying herself so much that she nearly forgot that they were here for a purpose. "Okay, remember what I said. Stick with the price you want to pay for it, and don't take the first amount he puts out there."

She didn't want anything in the box he was trying to sell off, and neither did anyone else, it seemed. As the bidding didn't generate even a buck, he added another box, then another. The box next, the one with the office things in it, was something she was interested in. When Booker leaned down and whispered in her ear, all thoughts of bidding flew out of her head.

"You'll have to take them all—remember that when you buy a bunch of boxes." She nodded, and when the auctioneer said a dollar, she raised her hand. While she had no idea what was in the boxes that she'd want, the office equipment appealed to her. Someone put their hand up, but he was only waving at someone across from him. The auctioneer asked him to conduct his conversations elsewhere and looked at her.

"You won, missy." She jumped for joy. Laughing, she went to the auctioneer and hugged him before she realized what she was doing. Telling him it was her first auction and bidding, he laughed with her. "Well, I'm glad you came here today. Thanks for the hug too."

When she started to go for her boxes, Booker told her to wait. No one would bother with them. He purchased the next lot of eight boxes, and she bought two more at the end that were filled with glasses, as well as wine glasses that she really liked. The two of them, she thought, had gotten a lot of junk with their stuff.

They started a pile by one of the trees. Booker even purchased a chair so she'd have something to sit in under the tree. When the rest of the boxes were sold off, her buying two more lots for a total of ten, the other Wilkersons joined them. They had twenty minutes before the bidding began on the furniture.

"Are you having fun?" She told Abby she was having too much fun, she thought. She didn't know how she was going to get everything in her car. "Don't worry about that. I called Mars, and he's going to rent one of those hauling things to bring our stuff home in. I missed the box lots, but I see you didn't. Would you mind if I went through them with you? Just to look at the things people consider junk?"

"I'd love that." Booker bought her lunch, as well as two bottles of water. The house, it seemed, wasn't selling for much, and she watched Booker when he decided it would be a good investment. Charlie moved closer to him when he started to tense up when the bidding started. "You can do this."

He only glanced at her, but she could see that he was happy she'd said that. His face not only relaxed, but he wasn't fisting his hands either. Putting her smaller hand into his much larger one, she felt like she was centered. It was a strange way to feel with only just meeting the man.

Booker bought the house, or so they all thought. Since it had gone well under what they should have gotten for the place, the auctioneer had to speak to the family. Booker kissed the back of her hand when he was asked to wait until the auctioneer returned.

"Thank you." She told him he was welcome and that he had calmed her as well. "We'll go to the furniture next. Are you ready for that?"

"I believe I am." She watched as the household things were brought out where the boxes had been. The big bed that came with several pieces of furniture caught her eye. Admiring it from a distance, she watched as others went over the stuff like they were searching for something special in it. "Are they serious about buying it for that price? I've heard that some of them are only willing to go to less than a hundred dollars. That seems cheap to me."

"They're putting that out there so that others around, like you, would hear it. They want you thinking it's not worth all that much. But I've seen it in the bedroom before you got here, and it's well worth a thousand or more. It's very old and made of mahogany. It looks to me like it might have been handmade right here on the property. That is a really good piece." She nodded but didn't go near the bedroom set. She didn't have the kind of money that would justify her paying that much for just a bedroom suite. Charlie did have her inheritance, but she was saving that for a rainy day. Booker laughed when she told him that. "My aunt would have told you that there are forever going to be rainy days, and you won't be able to save for all of them. What you should do is make each day count so that when the rainy day does come, you have your comfort in the things you did when you had the money and time."

"I think I might have liked your aunt." Booker kissed her then. Just a quick kiss on the mouth. "That was nice. Booker, I'm beginning to like you a great deal. Is that odd?"

"No. It's the way it should be. Come on, let's get us a place to bid on the things that we want. If you want the bedroom suite, then you get it. I'll even help you pay for it if it comes to being close to your limit." It didn't bother her that he was willing to do that. For some reason, it seemed right that they purchased the set together. Shaking her head at the nonsense in it, she moved to the group of people that had gathered around not just the bedroom suite but the table and chairs that had been brought out as well. "That is beautiful. Don't you think?"

"It is." A thought popped into her head in that moment. Of him sitting at one end of the table and her at the other, with people seated down either side with children in their arms. The thought, or vision, was so vivid that her breath caught when she realized this was their children and grandchildren. "Booker, something isn't right about this."

"I know." She had a feeling he did know, and she nodded too. "We'll figure things out when we get back home. All right. Today, let's just fill out our home."

She nearly missed bidding on the bedroom suite. Her mind was filled with words like home. Our. Even the vision of them and a large family. When Booker poked her in the ribs, she looked at the auctioneer when he started the bidding out at six thousand dollars.

When he got back down to a hundred dollars, a man in the crowd behind her said, "Here." She didn't turn and glare at him as she wanted to do but kept her eye on the man doing the fast-talking. Booker told her to wait to see where it went and if anyone was going to bid with them. When he told her now, she lifted her hand up to bid one-fifty.

The man behind her moved up to where they were standing. She saw him out of the corner of her eye and didn't like that he was staring at her. When Booker moved between the two of them, she felt better. The man started cursing quietly at first, then he started getting a little louder.

"Nothing is going to happen to you, love. All right? Just do what you're doing, and it'll be all right." Then the man shoved Booker into her. It wasn't a light push either. Both of them nearly tumbled to the ground. "Excuse me. You nearly knocked us down."

The man bumped Booker in the chest with his belly. Then he started talking to him in another language. While she had no idea what was being said, Booker did and was talking to the man calmly and without raising his fists up like the other man was.

"Hey. Hey now. What's all this about?" Booker told the auctioneer that the man had insulted his wife. Had called her a slut, and said that she only wanted the bed to entertain other men on. "He said that to you? What the hell — pardon me, ma'am — but what the hell is he being upset about? It's only an auction."

The man said something else, and Booker looked at the auctioneer. There were some very tense-filled moments there while neither of them spoke as the man went on and on about something. Not only did Abby join them, but all the Wilkersons stood up behind them.

"Mars, are you with this group?" He said he was. That this was his family. "This isn't right. Not to you or anyone in your family. But to be insulting like this to a pretty woman is just beyond what I think is right."

"I agree, Mr. Shadow." He asked the man to leave, and he just stood there, staring at her. Finally, when she'd had enough, she pushed her way in front of

Booker, and he put his hands gently on her shoulders.

"You're a nasty bully." She asked Booker to translate for her. He said that he understood what she was saying. "You are the meanest man I've met. We were all having a good time until you had to get all up in arms about a bedroom suite. What is the matter with you? Don't you have any man—?"

The blow to her face knocked her back. She not only saw stars, but she was sick with the pain of it. Closing her eyes when it became too much for her, Charlie wondered what her mother would say to her now. She'd think it was funny, she'd bet. There were noises going on, cursing too, but in the end, she just let go. Letting the pain take her under so that she'd not feel it for a while.

~*~

Wats was as pissed off as he'd ever been. Someone had actually hit a woman because she was bidding against him. Every time he thought about him hitting Charlie, he had to stop what he was doing and take a deep breath.

"This will go a good deal faster if you would just let your wife fix me up." He said he knew that, but he was safer in here. "Why? The guy was arrested, you told me."

"But I know where they took him." Charlie

laughed, then moaned. "I'm sorry you were hurt. But if it's any consolation, you got the bedroom suite for nothing."

"Booker told me." She looked around, then back at him. "May I ask you a question? You don't have to answer, but please don't make fun of me. All right?"

"Yes. But you should know that I don't lie. If you ask me something, you'd better be prepared for the answer. Ask me." She did. He had to think about his answer hard before he answered her. "You're worried that you're falling in love with my cousin? How is that something I'd make fun of you about?"

"I've only just met him today. I mean, literally today. He's kind and wonderfully sweet. He doesn't rush into things. Nor does he, and this is a biggy, treat me like I'm some sort of bimbo that he needs to protect." He laughed with her. "I suppose looking at me, you'd think I do need a protector. But he didn't shove me out of the way when I went to talk to the man. I know it was a stupid thing for me to do. I mean, I should have let someone handle it for me, but he didn't do anything."

"Actually, he did." She asked him what he was talking about. "My wife can't come here and take care of you because she's taking care of Booker. He has a broken wrist as well as needing stitches in both his lip and his hand. He knocked the man to his ass with one blow. He came up with a gun, believe it or not. But Booker didn't back down, he— Where are you going? I still need to stitch you up."

"Where is he?" Wats followed her, but not too closely. He could tell that she was pissed off, and he didn't want to come between her and her anger. "Booker Wilkerson, where the hell are you?"

He yelled that he was here, so she went to find him. As soon as they entered the room he'd been put in, Wats cringed. It was going to take him longer to heal from his wounds than it would Charlie, of that he was sure. Charlie asked him if he had a brain injury that she needed to be made aware of.

"Not that I'm aware of, no." Wats noticed that everyone seemed to leave them alone except him and Rayne. He was staying for the fun—he had no idea why Rayne was. "I was mad that he hit you."

"I was too, but you should have let the police handle it when he pulled out a gun." Booker looked at him, then back at Charlie. She did the same but looked at Booker. "What? Something you're not telling me."

"He was going to kill you." Charlie looked at Wats again. At his nod, she turned to Booker again. "I was willing to let the police handle it. I was sure that if I started on him, I would have killed him. But he pulled out the gun with the intention of killing you. He announced to everyone that you were one dead slut."

Booker stood up and made his way to Charlie. When she went into his arms willingly, Wats asked if they could finish stitching them up. They didn't want the swelling to get too much before they could get that done.

"I missed getting that table for our house." Wats didn't say anything about what Charlie said, but he did glance at his own wife. "This is so unfair. My very first auction and I have to get next to some dummy head that had to ruin it all for me."

"They stopped the auction." Charlie asked Rayne what she meant. "No one here wanted to go on without you there. The police are still here, of course, but the others voted to wait to see if you were going to join them again. The people here, they're really impressed with the two of you."

"We didn't do anything." Wats told her what he'd seen. "Okay, we did take on a bully, but we wouldn't have had to if he'd been a nicer person. What did he say to you?"

Booker said it wasn't nice, and wanted to leave it at that. Wats was sure that Charlie was going to push it, but she laid down on the bed that Booker was on so she could be stitched up as well. It took them more time than it normally would have because the two of them were talking to each other. Wats thought he was seeing the first blossoms of love.

When they were released to go back to the auction, people cheered for them. A couple of women told Booker he could defend their honor anytime he wanted. It was embarrassing to him. Wats could tell. Everyone was good-natured about it, and the police asked if they could talk to the two of them when the auction was over. Wats was very proud of his family right then.

Mars said he'd bid for them, but Charlie declined. She said her fun had been delayed, and she wanted to get back into it now. But she kissed him on the cheek for being so sweet, and then she turned to the auctioneer, asking him if he was ready.

"Yes, ma'am, I am. I have to tell you, I was never so terrified in my life as when that man said he was going to kill you. I thought for sure my heart was gonna stop when that husband of yours just stood up and knocked his gun away. Goodness." Charlie thanked him. "My wife, she said she's going to be watching for you from now on. You surely do get the job done when someone is nasty to you."

There was some fun made when Charlie bid

on the dining set. They teased them both about being careful not to bid against them. As was Booker's nature, he got a kick out of it and didn't anger. Wats only then realized it was the first time he'd truly ever seen his cousin pissed. He was usually one that would just walk away. This was a first for all of them today.

Not only did she win the dining set, but she also was able to bid and get two more bedroom suites. He wasn't sure, but he thought he'd found someone that loved auctions as much as Booker and Aunt Holly had. She was getting good at knowing when to stop, too.

As they were loading up the things on the truck Wats had gotten, Booker asked him for something for his headache. After checking him out, he told him he wanted some pictures of his head if he didn't mind. When he agreed, that worried him just a little, but Booker assured him it was only a headache. Uncle Josiah showed up just as the auction was coming to an end.

"There you are." Booker shook hands with the auctioneer and told him he ran a good auction. "You're a good man to have around. I don't suppose you have yourself a shop, do you? I mean, the way your missus was buy—"

"Missus?" Uncle Josiah looked around, then at his son. "Oh, yes. All right. But we do need to talk about some things later, son. All right?"

Uncle Josiah looked confused, but he wasn't going to embarrass them by asking questions now. Charlie asked him what he had in mind when the auctioneer asked about the shop.

"Well, you see all this stuff that people leave behind? Some of it is worth a little bit. A lot of it they just leave behind because they've realized they don't have the room to take it with them. I need someone I can call on to come and pick it up for me, and I'll pay you to do it. It won't be a lot, mind you, but a couple of dollars a box should cover you coming and getting it. If you've got a mind to."

Booker looked at his dad. "Will you go into partnership with me, Dad? I've decided I've had enough of teaching for a while, and I want to do something different. With you." Uncle Josiah looked like he was going to cry, and Wats patted him on the back. "We just purchased a house that I think will be perfect for odds and ends. My wife here is a doctor now, so she can afford to keep me in pocket money."

"I'd love nothing more." While Wats didn't know what house Booker was referring to, everyone was happy all the way around. "But first, I'd like for you to get to the hospital. The police said they'd make sure that the bill was paid by that moron."

"Do you want this to start now, Mr. Shadow?" Wats had forgotten the man's name and was glad that Charlie knew it. "We have enough help here today to load this up if you want. I mean, if that's all right with the rest of you."

"I have a better idea." Mars looked at Booker, then at him. "You go to the hospital with these two and make sure they're all right. The rest of us will do the clean-up and take it where you want."

"I bought this house. I think it will be perfect for where we can start out." They began to take the boxes and other things into the truck while he and Rayne loaded the two of them up in his car. He was beginning to worry about Booker, as he was too agreeable to going. He was going to keep him overnight just to make sure, no matter what the X-ray told them.

The ride to the hospital was quiet. He could hear Charlie and Booker talking to each other, but they were too quiet for him to hear. When Rayne took his hand into hers, he looked over at her.

"She loves him." Wats said he could see that too. "I think he loves her as well. He surely has taken a beating for her if he doesn't."

"They'll be all right, don't you think?" She asked him if he was worried about Booker. "Yes. He's not himself. I'm worried that there is something more wrong with him. I only checked his head. What if he was hurt elsewhere? I'm going to keep them both overnight, even if I have to beat the two of them into submission." Rayne agreed with him. And that made him more worried than he'd been before.

~*~

Rayne read the X-rays three times before she was satisfied with the results. Not that she was happy with what she saw, but she knew they were lucky that she and Wats had brought them into the hospital. Charlie had a concussion and two broken ribs, more than likely from falling over when hit. Wats joined her just as she was going to go see Charlie.

"He was shot. The shithead was shot, and he didn't say a word about it." Rayne asked how bad it was. "He was shot. Bad enough that I'm worried."

"You're worried because he's your relative. Tell me what you really think, like he's no relation to you." Wats said it was serious, but not that bad. "Good. She has a concussion. So getting them to stay will be easier since they'll both be here."

"I have him going into surgery now. I can't join him there, but I can be with him when he gets out. He also has a concussion and four broken ribs. I'm sure he's also got a couple of broken fingers." Rayne said he was a good man. "What do you mean? He was shot and didn't tell anyone."

"He didn't want to freak you out. Or, for that matter, Charlie." He'd not thought of that. "Would you have let them stay there had you known? I wouldn't have. But Charlie got to have a good time, and her day wasn't totally ruined by that man. Booker was a good man in being stoic and not worrying her or any of us too much."

"You know, he's always been like that. I remember once him having a broken hand during a football game." She asked how he'd gotten it. "He was the quarterback. I guess he was too good, and the other team thought they could take him out. But he played the rest of the game and even won before he let on that he was injured. I should have remembered that."

Rayne went to tell Charlie that she was spending the night. Wats told her that Booker was going to be fine but that he'd sustained a larger issue. Charlie had to threaten his life before he finally told her what had happened. She sat there for several moments without speaking, only to look at them with tears in her eyes.

"He said he loved me. We only met today, but it seems right. I don't know what to do about it. I mean, we only just met." Rayne asked if she loved him. "Yes. I don't know how that happened either, but knowing what he did for me today makes me love him all the more. Does that make sense to you?"

"Absolutely. It's the same thing for Wats and I." Rayne sent Wats on an errand while she sat on the side of the bed with Charlie. "He's going to be fine, you know. And if he won't behave, one of the others will sit on him until he does."

"Wats asked me to be his partner in his office. Are you going to be all right with that?" Rayne told her she was, that she was family now. "I guess I will be. Josiah, he was certainly confused. But he was really nice about not giving us up about the lie. It was nice, too, being called Mrs. Wilkerson."

"It is. Very nice. And you couldn't be joining a better family." Rayne called in the staff to make sure they started an IV for her, and told her that she'd let her know when Booker was out. Then when she left Charlie to her nurse, she stopped at the desk and asked if they could put Booker into the room with Charlie. "They'll be roaming the halls if you don't."

"We can arrange that, Dr. Wilkerson. My goodness, there are going to be a lot of you Wilkersons around here, aren't there? We'll have to make sure we use your initials, or we'll all be messed up." Rayne nodded and left to find Wats. It was the first time she'd been called Doctor Wilkerson by staff. It felt damned good.

As they waited for Booker to come out of surgery, Rayne made a couple of phone calls. One to her aunt to let her know where they were, and the second call to Josiah. He had asked her to call when they found out anything. He told her that he'd be right there. Wats went home to get Louis so that he could hang out with the others. He was becoming a wonderful part of the family quickly.

Rayne's phone rang, and she almost didn't answer it. Her aunt had called her several times over the last few days, and she wasn't ready to talk to her yet. But this time, armed with her anger that her newest family members had been hurt, as well as liking Charlie, she answered the phone with her title and Wilkerson.

"Where is Selma?" Rayne asked who it was, knowing full well that it was Aunt Becky. "Don't be a smart ass. Tell me where that sister of mine is. I have a mind to give her a piece of my mind."

"I'm sure you couldn't afford to give her any of your mind. You have seemed to lost your marbles anyway if you think that she's going to forgive you for treating her and me the way you did." Becky snorted. "You think I'm kidding? I'm not. I'm happy. I have children that I love and Aunt Selma to talk to when I need an adult. You were never there for me. While you didn't beat me, you were so verbally abusive to me that it made me feel like shit all the time."

"I kept you in line." This time she snorted. "Where is she? I want to know why she's changed the locks on our house. I need to get in and get some things out of it."

"Not without the police and Aunt Selma there you're not. Besides, it's not 'our' home. It's Aunt Selma's. She told me how you moved in with her like she needed you." Aunt Becky said she had. "Nope. Aunt Selma is a good deal stronger than you've ever given her credit for. Besides, I'm thinking you need to find yourself a home anyway. She's selling that one soon."

"Why would she—? You did that, didn't you? Just to see me on the streets. Well, I have money, so I can buy any home I want. You just wait and see." Rayne told her she didn't care if she had a house or not. "What a rude person you've turned out to be. My goodness, I should probably have beaten you once or twice to get that nastiness out of you. You should be nicer to me. I'm the only relative you have besides Selma. Did she tell you that she's dying? Well, she is."

"We're all dying, Aunt Becky. And you both being in your seventies isn't a big stretch in knowing that you're going to die too. But if you mean the cancer, yes, she told me about it. She also told me she's in remission. I have a feeling you would have left that part out had I not heard." Nothing. Not a denial or anything. "By the way, Grandda is fine as well. He's been having fun with our children. He said it makes him feel decades younger to be a great grandda."

"He should have died long ago, the old buzzard. He's just hanging on because he wants one of us to die first." She thought that was as good a reason as any and told her aunt that. "Have you always been a terrible person, or am I just noticing it?"

"Always have been. Always will be." She saw the surgeon coming down the hall. Charlie was just joining them in a wheelchair when he stopped to talk to them all. "I have to go. I'm not asking you for permission to hang up, Aunt Becky, because I know you well enough to not allow it. But I'll talk to you some other time."

Simply closing the connection, she stood up when Doctor Moran Davis sat across from Charlie. Since he and everyone else was going on the notion that she was Booker's wife, he was going to speak to her first.

"He's come through well. The bullet didn't do much damage. But he will need to rest up and behave himself for the next week or so. He had a lot of injuries and is lucky his head is hard." He looked at Wats. "I did take a look at his head. You're right. It was a good sized gash. I opened it up while I was in the sterile room and washed it out while I had him under. I hope you don't mind that I did that."

"No. I'm glad you did it. I don't want anything to happen to him." Wats looked relieved. "I was concerned when he wasn't arguing with us about bringing him in. He's not one to go to the doctor all that well."

"Well, he's in good hands, I believe." Doctor Davis looked at Charlie. "I'm to understand that you're going to be a physician here as well. You need anything, Charlie, you just let me know. I'm new as the head of this department, and I'm trying to make my way into getting things on a better standing between doctors and nurses. If you need anything, I'm serious, you just call me or come by."

It was another hour before they got to see Booker. Rayne could tell he was in a great deal of pain, so when he was taken to his room, sharing it with Charlie, she rushed the rest of them out of the room so he could get some meds and rest. Yes, Rayne thought this was a good family to be in with.

Louis was holding Wesley's hand when he got off the elevator. It was a good sight to see, the two of them. When he saw her, he came to her slowly. As soon as he was close enough, she gave him a big hug, then pulled out her phone to show him what they'd gotten for him today.

"The bunk beds will be nice if you want to have someone stay over. And look at this old flag. I thought if you wanted to, you could hang it on your wall." He looked at the pictures as she showed him, and she knew he had questions. "If you don't like it, Louis, we can sort that out later. I just thought bunk beds would be nice for your new room."

"Are you going to send me back?" She asked him where she'd send him. "To my dad. He will come and get me. I don't ever want to go back there again. I like having stuff I can wear that is clean and stuff."

"I like you being there with us too, Louis. But in answer to your question, no, he's not going to get you again. They found your momma. Did you hear that?" He nodded. Louis had told the police that she had been buried in the back yard near the apple tree. "And Brenda is in jail too. They'll never get by any of us to get to you again. I swear to you on my life."

He played with her badge while he stood there next to her. She didn't rush him. The teachers she'd spoken to about Louis said he was a thinker and that if someone rushed him, he'd tighten up tighter than a rubber band around a wrist. When he did look up at her, she smiled at him when he grinned.

"Grandpa Wesley said him and me would go fishing. I've never been, but when he told me he'd not been in years, I thought for sure he was kidding me." Rayne couldn't imagine the man with a fishing pole in his hand. "He told me if I wanted to, and I got good grades, him and me could have a lot of first times together. He even wants to go camping with me. I've slept outside before. I don't think it'll be the same with him, do you?"

"No. I'm sure you're going to have all the things necessary to make it a safe and fun trip. You might even make your food over an open fire." He warmed to that idea, then looked at her pictures again. "Do you not want the bunk beds?"

"No. I want them. That way, when Grandpa Wesley comes to read to me, we can rest up in the same room. He's pretty tired when he leaves me at night." She'd known Wesley was reading to Louis, just not that it had been nightly. "I'll be a really good boy for you, Mrs. Wilkerson. I promise you."

"I know that, Louis. But not too good, all right? I mean, we have to be able to ground you to the house so we can spend more time with you once in a while." She tickled him until he yelled for mercy.

When Wats joined her in their talk, she went to check on Charlie. She woke her up, she thought. "I'm sorry."

"Don't be. I was watching Booker." Coming into the room when asked, she stood by the bed so she could see how Charlie was doing. "I think my mom wouldn't be the least bit surprised that I fell for a Wilkerson. I mean, sheesh, she surely did talk about them a great deal. I'm so happy I'm going to be a part of this family that I could bust."

"I know how you feel." They both watched Booker breathing. "I just learned that you're going to have to keep an eye on Booker. He's sometimes a little stubborn when he's hurt and won't go to get checked out. They all have stories about him doing that."

"I will." Charlie took her hand into hers. "Thank you." Rayne asked her for what. "Not treating me like I wasn't good enough for him. For welcoming me to the family with open arms. I can't believe it's only been a few days, but I feel like I've known you all forever. It's a wonderful feeling."

"It really is."

She sat there with Charlie for a little while longer. As her eyes finally closed, she checked on Booker and left them there. She was glad to have a family like this one. Rayne would be on her toes to keep them healthy and well, but she was looking forward to that as well.

Chapter 1

Booker set another box on the table. He hadn't any idea how he'd been talked into doing this today, but now that he was here and working, he did feel better. Staying at home cooped up in the house wasn't doing his body any good. He had been feeling a great deal better, but he'd been sort of down in the dumps and he had no idea why.

Charlie had been living in the house with him now for the last few days, pampering him. Perhaps just a little too much, he supposed. But this morning she'd returned to work, and he was lonely. Then about noon, Charlie had called and asked him to go and see about the box lots they'd gotten. And to take his dad.

The two of them had been working on the boxes for nearly two hours now. Booker didn't want to admit he was having fun, but he was. Just finding things, looking them up to see not just what they were used for, but if they had much in the way of value, was enjoyable. Especially since he was getting to spend so much time with his dad.

"Would you look at this? I've not seen one of these in a long time. Look, Booker." He turned to look at what his dad had. Taking it from him when offered, he rolled the beautiful glass ball around in his hand to see all the beautiful colors. "I think that's a paperweight. In my day that was something everyone had on their desks. However, I'm thinking that is older than mine were, even back then, and much prettier. What do you think?"

After handing it back to him, Booker looked it up. "Dad, they are expensive if they're old. However, I have no idea how to tell if this one is old or not, do you?" They looked all over it for markings, but only found that no matter how they turned it, it was still beautiful. "Look at this. It says here that this design is called French art. The flowers look almost real. Like they put them in the glass before sealing it up."

"There are four more of them here too." They marveled at the design in each piece. Even when they found two with the same sort of design in them, they were as different as night was to day. One of them was larger than the other three, but still as beautiful. However, instead of simply flowers, this one had what appeared to be hard candy inside of it. The colors were outstanding too. "Did all these come from the same auction?"

"No. Several, as a matter of fact. We have a deal with all the auctioneers that they can bring by the things that don't sell and put them in the barn. Then when Charlie or I come around, we bring them into the house. Especially the smaller boxes that need to be sorted through. I've been having a crew come out and clean up the furniture when it comes in. They also decide if it's worth keeping or not." He picked up the notes he had on this auction. "Mark Windermere. He brought three pieces of furniture, as well as fourteen boxes of left behind stuff. I guess this is from there."

They looked through the rest of the box lots and found four more, for a total of eleven glass paperweights. He wasn't sure he wanted to sell them because they were so beautiful. Dad suggested asking Charlie if she wanted them for her office at home. A place she was still setting up.

"That reminds me. She wanted to know if you wanted to live with us. I was telling her that I had no idea why I bought such a big house, and she said it was for you to live with us. Don't feel any pressure, Dad, to do so, but it would be nice to have you hanging around with us. Charlie said she was enjoying having you around to talk to as well." Dad said he'd think about it. He didn't want to intrude. "If I thought you'd be an intrusion, Dad, I would have said so. You have to know me well enough to know I speak my mind."

"You do at that. So does Charlie. But you two are just starting to get to know each other, and I'd not want to be in the way. What would I do? However, son, to be honest with you, I really like living alone. No one to keep me on my toes and such. I might change my mind when the kids come around, I do want to be around them. But honestly, I really like where I'm staying for now. Thanks, son." He nodded. "I do like doing this with you, however. I get you all to myself for a change. Not that I don't adore Charlie. She can light up a room just by stepping into it. I'm glad to be working with you and this project. I'll get to know all the things you've learned about auctioning as well."

"Aunt Holly certainly loved it. She could dicker a deal better than anyone. I don't get a lot for these box lots that are brought to me to resell, but she'd get a kick going through each box like you are. She'd also be warning us about washing up after each boxload. She was big on that." Booker laughed as he pulled a chair over for him to use to look into the box he had. "Once, she and I were on a road trip. I don't know if they still do it or not, but there was this sale of sorts that went down the highway, and you'd just go from vendor to vendor to get what you wanted. It wasn't as much fun as going to an auction, so we only went that one time. But the very next weekend, we were headed to the next big one."

"Did you ever find anything that was valuable?" Dad had taken a chair too, so they were about eye level when Booker nodded. That was when he noticed that he and his dad had the same color eyes. He'd not been this close to his dad too much before now. "Tell me about it. It would be like hitting the lottery, I would think."

"It was for us. We'd picked up a lot of really old and out of date magazines. The auctioneer would usually just tell us to take them if they were next to a box of stuff we bid on. Like glamour magazines that would still be in pretty good shape. If I remember correctly, they were from the early nineteen hundreds. A few too from the late eighteen hundreds. We'd only take them to look at the articles in them. The prices of things. You know, a bit of history you'd not get in a classroom. So once we got them home, we looked at each one of them like they were masterpieces someone had treasured. After we'd gotten our enjoyment out of them, we put them on one of those bidding sites and sold them off. For a great deal more money than we spent at the auction we'd gotten them from." Dad asked him what he'd sell the balls for. "I'm not sure. Perhaps I'll put one of them on that site and see what it brings. It might be fun to know that someone is bidding on them too." Dad picked out the one they were going to start on. Opening his phone to the app, Booker realized he needed to ask Charlie first if she wanted it. Sending her a picture got a phone call from her. She asked him if he was shopping or working. They all three laughed. "We found them in a couple of boxes that were left behind. I was going to put one of them on an auction site, but thought I'd ask you first if you wanted it for your desk."

"Do you have anything with more green in it? I'm partial to that color." He sent her pictures of all eleven of them, and she picked out the two she wanted. He asked her if she was all right. "Yes. I love working with Wats. He's the kind of doctor I want to be. Also, get this — we'll close up at lunch time and go out to eat. Still on call, but at least we have an hour to unwind. How's your day going so far?"

"Great. Dad and I have been separating out the things we want to sell from the things we want to donate. Which is more than you might think." He laughed when she did. "We do have a lot of one ofs, they're called. One dish. A mug that isn't chipped.

Stuff not worth it, I guess."

"I think maybe I did figure that was going to happen about us finding singles of things. With no one taking it with them when they left the auction, I guess it wouldn't be something easy to figure out. Someone here gave me an idea too. That we need to make up single packs. She said there are a lot of people out there that don't need a set of dishes starting off. One of each thing, like my mom had, would more than likely be all they need. Mom had a single plate she used, with a bowl for her cereal. Mostly what she ate when she wasn't eating out, I guess."

He could hear Wats tell her that her patient was there, and they all three laughed when he teased her about missing him. Booker missed her as well. He wanted to stop the world from going on so he could spend some time getting to know Charlie.

Dad and he had gone through about half the boxes when they decided to have lunch themselves. Locking up the house, he made sure the barn was devoid of things people might want to take, and they left. The diner was open for business, but it didn't seem to be all that busy. As they looked around Booker could see the place needed a major overhaul. Seats and tables for the most part.

He and Dad talked about some of the

improvements they'd make to this place if they were owners. It would also be a good place to sell off some of the things they had in the house. Using the plates, for one thing, but also the odds and ends tables they had that had no matches. Dad said he'd even put some of the plates on display with a price tag on them.

As they were finishing up their meals, the cook came to sit with them. "Benson Tayler." They shook hands. "My wife, your waitress today, overheard some of the things you were talking about to make improvements on this place. I like them."

"We were just funning around, to be honest with you." Benson nodded and looked around. Booker did as well. "You want to go into partnership with us on this?"

"No. I want to sell out. For a song too. I'm sick of getting up early every morning and having to come here. My wife and I have been running this place for the last fifteen years, and we're hoping to have us some fun before we're too old to enjoy life." Benson laughed. "We'll sell it cheap and walk away. I have no plans to ever change my mind."

After working out the details, Dad asking a great many questions about it, they decided to take the offer. Dad called Uncle Aidan to have him work up a contract, and it was a done deal, minus any last-minute changes. They were still sitting there when Charlie joined them. She looked like she'd had a good day today. After kissing her, he asked her about it.

"I did have a good day, as a matter of fact. We shared the load, which I was grateful for. And we made a plan that will have us both seeing the patients so they can be familiar with us when they come in to see us." She pulled the half of his sub he'd not eaten toward her and finished it off while she continued. "The last patient needed to see him, so he told me to come meet you here. Also, your cousins are coming to help you with the sorting. I think they want to find the next big treasure or something."

"We did find something with the glass balls." Dad explained to her what they'd done to put it on an auction site. "I don't know much about them, but it certainly was a great deal of fun for me to help out with. Also, should it sell, Booker said he'd put the rest on there and use the money toward buying more things for the shop."

"Used Things is what you're going to call it, I heard." Booker laughed as he explained it was up for debate. "No, I like it. It says just what it is. A place for used things."

Not only did his cousins show up, but his uncles as well. As the uncles and his dad talked about the restaurant — they were excited to get going on it — he and his cousins talked about the boxes of stuff, as well as the furniture. Brandon was looking for a large desk he could use to put his work on.

Booker overheard his dad saying they should take turns working the restaurant in pairs to be able to get out more. It seemed like a good plan, but none of them knew the first thing about running a restaurant. But they'd learn together, of that he had no doubt. Mars asked him what he thought about them taking over.

"Nothing. Go for it is all I can say. I was going to ask if they wanted to run the used place too. This way they could take turns as well. Not that it needs to be open every day, but that would be something we'd have to work out, I suppose. I want to run it too, but not full time. I need to find something that challenges me every day, and emptying boxes might not be it. I think, as Dad said, it would be a good thing to get out in the world again. Besides, if it makes them happy, then I'm happy."

The uncles and his father had lived a pretty sheltered, strict life up until their wives were gone. All of their spouses were dead now, and none of the uncles could have been happier. Even as he said it in his mind, he knew that had anyone heard him say that, they'd think him a monster. However, anyone that knew the women the senior Wilkersons were married to would understand precisely what he was talking about. Booker knew he was sleeping better at nights.

They got the house he'd gotten at the auction set up with the furniture they'd gotten as left overs in no time. Each room was just a hodgepodge of things scattered around, with what they thought was expensive mixed with the things that were cheap. The things he and Charlie had purchased were still in the big barn waiting to be cleaned and then put into their own house. Wats had a truck, as did Shawn, so they went to the barn behind Mars's house and began taking stuff out of it to put in Used Things as well. By the time dinner rolled around, they were starved and had the place looking good. The only thing he didn't know how to do was price things.

"I'll do that. I can look things up while I'm putting my feet up." Abby smiled at them as she rubbed her small belly. "The baby is draining me anyway, and this would be a good excuse for me to lie down. If I fall asleep while doing it, at least I'll feel better about napping all the time."

So they each had an assignment — more like they had suggested things they'd do — and he left with a happier heart. Even though he was still supposed to be taking it easy for a bit longer after being shot, he was looking forward to going home with Charlie and snuggling up on their new couch. As soon as they were home, they did just that, took a nap together on the only thing in the living room so far.

~*~

Charlie staggered her way to the bathroom when she woke up. She and Booker had been taking a great many naps over the last few days. She knew it had a great deal to do with the beating they'd both taken at the auction four days ago.

The man there had been really upset that she had wanted the same piece of furniture he did. After bullying her, calling her nasty names as well, the man had beaten her up and even pulled out a gun to kill her over it. None of the others had ever heard of something so drastic happening at an auction.

However, since she'd gone back to work, she was sure she'd be getting better at not being so tired all the time. As she was coming out of the bathroom, turning left instead of to the right back to the living room, she made her way to the kitchen. She'd nearly screamed when their cook of only two days asked her if she needed anything.

"Just a glass of tea if there is any made." She poured her a large glass and she drank it down almost as quickly as it had been poured. "I haven't any idea why I'm so thirsty or exhausted all the time."

"I'd say you're resting up because of what has happened to the two of you. The dryer weather, coming up on fall, will also make you thirsty. Being safe and in love, those are powerful ways to feel like you can just take a nap when the urge hits you." She smiled at Mrs. Mae. "I was going to ask you if you'd like some dinner, but it is getting late. What would you like to do?"

"Sandwiches if you don't mind. I'm hoping that tomorrow after work I can come back here and start putting my office together. Booker has his all set up, but I think he did it more out of boredom than anything else." They both laughed, and she kissed Booker when he joined them. "We're not having anything big for dinner. Is that all right with you?"

"Of course. I was thinking the same thing. We have been burning the candle at both ends since we met up." He stretched and sat down at the bar that had been part of the renovations to the big room. "I've gotten a great many of the boxes emptied and sorted out. Dad was a great help. And the paperweight is already being bid on. So you'll have to make sure you only want the two before we put them on there as well."

"I will look at them. To be honest, I don't know that I want them at all." She laid her head on his shoulder and yawned. "I have to go to bed early today, as I have to get to work by six to get my office set up before patients start to come in. Did I tell you the hospital is going to start sending patients our way if they don't have a doctor and their ailments can easily be fixed by us? It'll be nice being a little busy."

"Good for you guys. I'm meeting a couple of auctioneers at the house so they can drop off some things first thing in the morning. That way I can get a jump on the things we're going to put on that auction site."

When Booker yawned again, Ms. Mae sent them into the living room where they could put their feet up. That was the best idea anyone had ever given her, Charlie thought.

At some point she knew she was being carried up to bed. Even when she was laid on it, she knew she should at least move or thank Booker. When the bed shifted under her, moving with his weight being put on the bed, Charlie smiled to herself and let sleep take her under. Who knew that being hurt could be so tiresome?

Waking when her alarm went off, she laid there for a few seconds to take a quick inventory of her body. She certainly felt more rested. Reaching for Booker, she was dismayed to find his side of the bed not just empty, but cold as well. Getting up, she found Booker in the shower with soap in his hair and the room steamed up.

"Can I join you?" He told her while washing his hair that if she did, she'd be late to work. "I think we can work something out where we're both happy with a quickie, don't you?"

Stripping down, she was nearly tossed against the wall the moment she entered the stall. Booker's hands were all over her, and she tried her best to touch him as well. As soon as she wrapped her hand around his cock, he stopped moving and looked at her.

"I'm hard like this nearly all the time." She said she thought she'd have to start taking panties with her to change several times a day. "I need you, love. More than I think is even calculable."

When she nodded, Booker wasted no time in lifting her up and pressing her against the shower wall. The tile was cold, but only for a moment because he filled her. Crying out, having her body stretch for his size and thickness, neither of them moved for several seconds.

"I love you." She adjusted her body a little to make herself more comfortable when he told her to stop. "If you keep that up, I'm going to come long before you have had any fun. I know we said quick, but I want to savor you for a little bit."

He made love to her gently then. It was a wonderful feeling, having the man she loved more than life inside of her. When he kissed her, that too seemed to be filled more with love than a quick way to some relief. She came twice before he started taking her just a little more forcefully. By the time he was taking her harder, the room spinning on axes, it seemed, she came several more times, one right after the other.

"Come again for me, Charlie. Come and let me take you to a peak that will take us both under." She screamed this time, not even caring that she was going to have a sore throat later. Charlie came so hard that rainbows danced behind her closed eyes. Screaming a second time when he pounded himself empty inside of her, Charlie held onto him as if—and it more than likely did—her very life depended on it.

Neither of them moved for several moments. It could have been hours, she thought, because time had no meaning for her at that moment. Looking up at Booker when he kissed her on the cheek, his movement had her coming again. His laughter made her feel silly.

"I think at some point you and I are going to have to make love in a real bed. While this is wonderful, it wasn't enough. For me anyway. I want to explore your body from top to bottom. I need to feel you wrapped around me." She kissed him this time. "We need to get going or we'll both be in trouble."

They played around in the shower for the next twenty minutes. He washed her hair for her and she was in heaven. While she scrubbed his back, he told her what his plans for the day were. It was as if they'd been together forever, the two of them, the way she felt so at ease with him.

Getting dressed, her phone rang three times. It was Rayne's aunt. Rebecca could blow it out her ass for all she cared to talk to her about her friend. How she got her number was a mystery, but not one she would look into. Life was too short for that. When it started to annoy her, she simply blocked the number and went to the kitchen for some much needed food. They'd not eaten last night, and she was beginning to feel it.

"There are a couple of things I'll need to talk to you about this evening, if you don't mind." Booker asked Ms. Mae if he could help. "Yes, of course. Do you wish to have the groceries delivered or for me to make you a list to have picked up? I can order it too, if you'd show me how to do that."

"I can do that today. You'll need to have a

computer in here. Or at the very least a laptop to order from." She said she didn't need all that. "I think once you start to see all of my cousins and their wives coming around, you're going to have to hire out a semi to bring in the food. We can all put the food away."

"Well then, you set me up with it. I won't be ordering anything for myself. I want you to know that." Charlie told her she'd better be ordering food for herself. It was one of her perks. "Well now, ain't that the nicest thing. Thank you. My husband needs to have himself some small meals while he's at home waiting on me."

"Bring him here to eat with you, Mae." She said she couldn't do that, and Booker insisted. "That way, we'll get to know him as well. I don't suppose he's looking for a job, is he? While I don't mind driving myself, I'd really like for someone to drive Charlie to work and pick her up. At least until we can figure out what Rayne's aunt is up to. I don't want her hurt. And it wouldn't surprise me at all if she were to resort to hurting or taking one of us to get to Rayne."

"Oh, I never thought of that. From talking to Rayne, that does sound like something she'd do. My goodness, I cannot believe she's related to that wonderful old man. Yes, please. I could walk, but since I never know when I'm getting off or even what time

I'll get there—" She looked at her watch, a standard part of a nurse's uniform from times gone by. "I should be there in thirty minutes. So much for arriving early."

After kissing him on the mouth, she left him to his day. Calling his dad to meet him at the Used house, Dad came over to have some tea with him and plan out their day. Mars showed up too, along with North. He'd been the one that had written up the contract for the restaurant. They still needed a name, but Dad told him they were working on it now. Booker thought it was funny that they'd decided it was theirs now to do with as they pleased. Really, he didn't mind so long as, like he'd said, they were happy.

Booker had never seen his dad so happy. Not like this. He was also putting on some muscle, he'd noticed, when they were unloading furniture. All of them were, he supposed. Booker knew Dad had set himself up a few pieces of exercise equipment in his condo. Asking if he wanted help moving it out to the second bay of this garage, Dad said he'd never use the equipment then.

"It's right there when I get up out of bed. I make myself get on it and do the workout I was told I needed to start out with. I'm not seeing Wats for it, but someone who specializes in men our age that haven't experienced a day in their lives." Booker told him that was great. "I feel that way too. I don't get out of breath with every stair I climb. Not only that, but I'm enjoying eating things I never had the opportunity to before. I eat healthy ninety-five percent of the time, but I can also splurge when I've had a good week."

Booker and the rest of them had noticed their fathers walked a great deal more. Dad and Uncle Clayton had bikes they rode to and from town when the weather was better. Even when it wasn't, he'd see them out there having a good time. Booker was happy for it. With Uncle Clayton running for mayor, it was doing him a great deal of good getting out and about too. Things were going in a way their wives would never have approved of, Booker was sure of that.

"I've been meaning to tell you something, Booker. It's been something that—well, I have some things in a storage locker downtown. I think most of my brothers do as well. I don't know when it was I decided to put things in it that I didn't want your mother into, but I've had it for at least twenty or more years. I'd like you to help me clean it out if you don't mind." Booker asked his dad what sort of stuff was in it. "Nothing earth shattering. When I'd have to travel for one thing or another, I'd pick up little things. Things I knew your mother wouldn't approve to be in the house. Ornaments I've collected since I was a child. I had forgotten about those being in there until Charlie mentioned you two needing some. Also, there are larger things I found on little trips abroad. You and Charlie might like them."

So they set up a date to go and do it. As they pulled into the parking area for Used, Booker was surprised to see more than the few auctioneers waiting for him. While he wasn't late, he did tell them he was sorry for making them wait for them.

"Nothing to worry about, young man. We're here to see if you'd do the same for us. We've all been talking, and knowing there is a place that will take some of the things left behind will save all of us some money. Not having to rent a large dumpster would be one of the savings, not to mention, it's sort of a perk to some of the people buying that they don't have to take every little thing in a box." The man laughed. "Not that we'd be pawning crap over to you. No, nothing like that. But things like large pieces of furniture that don't sell simply because of its weight and size. The last two auctions I held had three armoires, as well as a lovely hide-a-bed couch. Those suckers are made to last, but they weight nearly a ton, it feels like."

After they agreed on a price for them to come and get the things, as well as setting them up, they decided all profits for selling the things would be the shop's. Dad and Uncle Aidan took three of the cousins with them to pick up what was still at the home of the auction that had happened just last night. This was going to either be the biggest bust in the world or something that might well be fun to run. Either way, the uncles and his dad were running with it, and they didn't care if they made a profit or not.

"The restaurant, did your dad tell you the name of it?" Booker asked North if it was bad. "No. Not even close. They want to have Abby come in and teach them the recipes Aunt Holly taught us, and they'll call it Holly's Place. The profit, which I'm betting will not be too bad, will be put toward the housing we're working on to get abused families away from their abuser."

Booker had to look away. Asking if Mars had heard made him cry just a little harder, and when Mars was told Booker had to leave the room, he'd been so touched. Not just for the name, North told him, but for the fact they were using the things she had cooked for them. Aunt Holly had been a fantastic cook, and the best mother any of them had ever had. Even only being their aunt, she had raised them well.

Aunt Holly would be busting their chops over this, but she'd be so proud of her brothers. They had changed so much in the last month that at times Booker had to remind himself this relationship with his dad wasn't decades in the making. That they'd been getting together only recently. It felt like forever, like his mother had never intruded. If his dad was there right now, he'd hug him so hard he was sure he'd squeak.

It took them an hour to gather up the previous owners of Holly's Place—the address they'd been given wasn't the correct spelling. Once the paperwork was signed over, they closed down—which wasn't all that hard since there wasn't anyone in the place—and called in a crew to have the place overhauled. The benches were pulled out first while the kitchen was being stripped down. Anything useable or refinishable, the crew was directed to put into Used Things. Reusing and resourcing was something they were very good at, thanks to their Aunt Holly.

"I was just thinking about how much we learned from Aunt Holly, and how it was never really a lesson, but just doing the things she did. One of them that comes to mind is how she would take printed paper, shred it up, and use it for stationary that she'd take to the nursing home. The pretty ribbon, she told me once, was something she'd pick up here and there from other things, then reuse them on the pretty paper she'd make." North laughed as he wrestled out one of the particularly bad benches from the restaurant.

"She'd even find a use for this sucker, even though I'm tempted to toss it out. However, I'm going to put it in the shop with the others so someone can come in and redo it if they want. Christ, I wish she was here more and more daily."

"Me too." Once the benches were pulled out, along with the tables, two men showed up to purchase them. They were, they told them, going to use them in the homemade drive-in hey'd set up in their barn for kids to use. Booker just gave them to him, for him giving the kids a little nostalgia for things past. "Word sure is getting around fast."

By the end of the afternoon, the restaurant was devoid of anything but the bar. They were going to hire someone to come in and clean it up after the new floors were put in. Dad, beginning to enjoy getting things set up for the place, called in a couple of favors, and not only got an ice cream freezer, but also a coffer maker, brand new, to have set up when it was ready to receive things like that. They were still laughing as they headed home for lunch.

Booker did some work while he was eating. The end of the year was coming up, and he wanted to get all his paperwork turned in. He wasn't going back the following term. His bosses weren't all that happy with him, but he didn't really care right now. He was going to do this for himself and Charlie. Booker decided he just wanted to be a lazy bum for a while, and be a househusband for Charlie when she came home from work. Booker thought he'd do a great job of it too.

Chapter 2

With her office set up the way she wanted at work, Charlie went to find Wats. She was glad that starting out she'd be able to ease into being a doctor. Also, she wanted to make sure he was happy with her being his partner in this. She didn't want to mess up with anyone.

He turned to her when she asked him if she was doing all right, for more than likely the hundredth time today. "Will you please just be a doctor?" Wats laughed. "Rayne is doing the same thing at the hospital, I heard. Falling all over herself trying to make up for the fact that she shouldn't be a doctor. Or something like that. Who knows. You're a doctor. You have the certificate to prove you were that good. Now, you have a list of patients the same as I do, and we're going to have fun. Once we're up with more people coming in, I know we're going to be the best office in the state.

What did you do with all your books?" She told him they were still boxed up, waiting on a shelf. "I think there might be some extra ones in the storage unit that Mars rented for us to take from and put in. We'll head there after work."

Her first patient was an elderly woman that had been brought in by her son. They looked like they could barely stand, but he was careful with her. She was for him too. If either of them fell it would be bad for the both of them, Charlie thought. Checking out the woman's lungs, she noticed that her skin was dry, and made a mental note to tell her son she needed to have lotion put there. The rest of the exam had her adding two more notes to the first one.

"All right, Ms. Millner, what has brought you in today?" She showed her the cut on her arm. "How long ago did you do this? It should have had stitches in it right from the start. No worries, we'll get you fixed up."

"You're a pretty little thing, aren't you?" Blushing, she thanked Ms. Millner. "I knew your momma. She was a beauty too. My goodness, she would make a man wet his drawers without a bit of trouble if he got mouthy with her in her courtroom. She ran that place with an iron fist, but she had a heart of gold, your momma did."

"I miss her a great deal. We were all we had for a long time, and now she's gone." Ms. Millner consented to having her arm stitched up. "I remember her talking about you and that son of yours once. Nothing terrible, but she said that if more parents raised their kids to be like Teddy out there, the world would be a great deal more tolerant of each other."

"Teddy is a good boy. Not as touched as they told me he'd be when I first birthed him. He can dress himself and me. Make us up one of them microwave dinner things when the people bring them by for us. He can even make some popcorn without burning the place down around our ears. I love him with all my heart." Charlie hugged her as she finished up with the ten stitches in her arm. "I know he ain't got no appointment or anything, but I was wondering if you or Wats can check him over. He don't complain too much, but his head has been nagging at him a bit more than usual. I worry about him."

When she had her arm wrapped up and in a sling so she'd not use it, forgetting about the stitches, Charlie went to find Wats. He was in his office on the computer when she asked him if he had time to look at Teddy.

"Yes. But his mom will have to be in there with me. He won't let me touch him without her permission. I don't know that anyone hurt him, but she has always been protective of him, and that is the only way I can be sure neither of us get hurt." She said she was finished with Ms. Millner and went to get Teddy. "Hello, Teddy. I saw you working at the grocery store the other day. You're doing a fine job, Mr. Jacobs said."

Wats joked around with the older man as he examined first his heart and lungs, then his ears. Pausing at his right ear then going to the left, Wats was talking to Teddy, but also her, when he asked to have the X-ray machine set up for some head X-rays.

"I'm going to take a couple of pictures of your head, Teddy. Will you be all right to sit still for me?" He looked at his momma. When she nodded, he did too. "Good. You've a bit of ear wax build up in there, and I want to make sure it's nothing else. Then, if you're up for it, we'll clean out your ears for you. You'll be able to hear better too."

"I have to listen to my shows with the headphones on high or it upsets my momma. Will this help me hear my shows?" Wats told him he hoped so. "I don't want to upset my momma. She's good to me, and she loves me."

"Of course I do, you old turd." They all four laughed, and Charlie left the room to get the area ready for Teddy. When she had it set up, she went to help Ms. Millner to the room. "Is he all right, you think? They told me when he was a baby that I'd be lucky to get ten years of him around. And he'd need constant care. We're all we have, you know."

"I can see that. And I will have Wats talk to you when he comes in. There is no sense in borrowing trouble, Ms. Millner. Just wait and things will be revealed when he's finished with the X-ray." She nodded then hugged her. "Not that I mind the hug, but what was that for?"

"Not treating me like an old woman that doesn't have the sense to get in out of the rain. That's why I don't go to the center anymore. Those girls running that place treated myself and Teddy like we was like that." She huffed. "You'd think when a person makes it to the ripe old age of ninety-nine, they'd treat her like she knows what is what."

"My goodness. Ninety-nine? I didn't look on your chart or I might well have asked you if it was a misprint or something. You have seen a thing or two, I'm betting. Wat's wife has her grandda that is ninety-three. James Oliver. His daughters, at least one of them, treats him like he's nothing more than a spot under their shoe. Good for you."

"Young people do that. I don't know that they

realize it most of the time. I know there are some out there that do, but for the most part, I think, anyway, that we've a few things to do before we pass on." They both moved out of the way when Teddy and Wats arrived. "I'll just have me a seat right here, son. I'll even old your hand if you'll be still for us. Then you and me will go and have a creamy chicken sammich at the little store."

The X-rays were finished in no time. True to his word, Teddy lay still and did what he was asked. When it was finished up, the films having been processed, Wats sat the three of them down and showed them what the X-ray was telling them.

"You have a wax buildup, Teddy. It won't take anything to have it taken care of right now if you're up for it." Teddy again looked at his mom before answering. "I'm going to have to put you under a little, Teddy. It's very delicate work, but your momma will be right here in the event you're worried about it. I'll have you up and moving around in no time."

"Momma?" Ms. Millner said she'd not leave him, and it would be good for him to be able to hear. "I know, but I don't want to be put in a dark place. Where are they gonna put me under?"

Wats explained what he'd meant, and Teddy was all right with it. As soon as she put an IV into his arm, Teddy was out seconds later. Wats, with her assistance, started on the procedure right away.

It took nearly an hour to clean out Teddy's ears. The right ear was impacted and had to have the most work done on it. The things that had attached themselves to the wax were nasty, and the lumps hard as stones. After getting his ears cleaned out and drops put into them, they allowed Teddy to sleep for just a little while longer.

"He's going to be fine, isn't he, Wats? I don't want him to be in pain anymore." Wats assured her that he was doing well. "I just don't know what I'd do without him. He's been such a good boy for me. Them X-rays didn't show a tumor or anything, did they? As I said, I don't want him to be hurting none if I can help it."

"He might have to adjust a little to having the buildup gone. But that won't cause him any pain, just something he's going to have to adjust to. Charlie and I will run a battery of tests on the blood she drew, but I don't foresee anything coming of it. Perhaps he could shed a few pounds, but that isn't a concern with him being as old as he is. You either, for that matter. Just try and make sure he's not eating too many sweets while he's watching his shows." She said he loved to have candy corn this time of year. "Don't let him overindulge too much."

When Teddy woke up, he sat there for a few minutes listening to them talking. The conversation changed from him to what was going on with the other places going in around town. Teddy smiled at his momma when she asked if he was all right.

"I sure can hear better. I don't have to turn up my headphones anymore." Ms. Millner told him that was wonderful. "Oh, Momma, it's like having new ears. Wats and his pretty friend gave me new ears."

After they left, Wats went back to his office and she returned to hers. There was a great deal of emotions going on since Teddy and his momma left. She, for one, was glad for the few minutes alone. She heard Booker talking to Wats in the waiting room as she sat there thinking about him. Leaving her office, she met the two of them in the hallway.

"I brought lunch for everyone. Dad and the others are having too much fun to want to break to go home, so after I delivered their meals, I brought you guys some as well." Charlie told him she was starving, and they made them up a little picnic in the break room for the three of them. Adeline, the secretary they'd hired recently, said she was going home for lunch with her hubby. The three of them devoured their club sandwiches like they'd not eaten for a month.

"That was wonderful, Booker. Thanks." Wats left them then, saying he had things he needed to finish up too. Booker took her hand into his and held it after kissing it.

"How are things going with what you had going today?" Booker told her about how he had ten more auctioneers that were willing to use him as an outlet. Also, there were some storage lockers he'd been given the key to so they could clean them out. He told her a few of the things they'd found so far. "Do you know how to fix a washer or dryer?"

"No. But there is a man at the nursing home that knows how to fix things like that. Dad knows him. He and some of his buddies from there are going to come by and see if they're fixable. If not, they'll tear them down for parts. They're also going to come in and run the vacuum for us, as well as tighten up some screws or whatever needs to be done to some of the things before they might be resalable." A patient came in while they were talking and Wats said he had it. "I'm hoping that at some point we're going to be able to sell off or give away this stuff, or we'll have a house full. But it's also generating a great deal of interest, and that's never a bad thing. If we can fix up a couple of things to help people get through some rough patches, I'll feel like it's all been worth it. How's your day going so far?"

"Not too bad." She told him about Teddy and his mom. "She'll be a hundred next summer, and Teddy will be seventy-seven. I think the love they have for each other is what has kept them going."

The noises at the front of the offices had them both standing up. She knew who it was without looking — Rayne's aunt Rebecca. When she busted into the room the two of them were in, she looked around like they were hiding Rayne from her.

"Where is she?" Booker asked her who she might be talking about. "My niece, damn it. Rayne Oliver. I know she's working here. Isn't that where all the nurses get their first job? A run down doctor's office? I need to talk to her. Call her in, or whatever you need to do to leave us alone in private."

"Doctor Wilkerson doesn't work here. I told you that three times while you were huffing and puffing your way back here. Have you seen your doctor lately? You look a little bit overweight, and your blood pressure is more than likely equal to your weight." Wats sat down with them as he continued to talk to them. "In the event you don't know her, this is the bad aunt of Rayne's. She's been trying to get in touch with my wife for three days now. To no avail, I might add."

"Don't you dare be discussing my weight. And my blood pressure is just fine, thank you very much.

I don't know this Wilkerson person. Who are you referring to?" Each of them raised their hands. "Not you idiots. Never mind. Point me in the direction of my niece and I'll be on my way."

"Your niece, a doctor and my wife, is working today, and I'm not going to tell you where she is so that you'll upset her." Rebecca sat down and Charlie could almost hear the chair groaning. When she asked again where she was, Charlie had a feeling her pressure was about to pop. The woman looked ghastly. "You don't look so good. In all seriousness, when was the last time you were— Shit, call an ambulance."

Rebecca just tumbled out of the chair she'd been in. Lucky for her that Wats was so close, or she might well have hit her head as she was going down. As it was, they were going to need help to get her up again. The woman had to be pushing at least three hundred and fifty pounds.

She and Wats took turns doing CPR on her until the medical team arrived with the ambulance. It was touch and go for a while until the medics were able to use the defibrillator to get her heart going again. As she was rushed to the hospital, Charlie knew it wasn't going to end well for the elderly woman.

~*~

Wats was going to assist on the operation that

was going to be needed for Rebecca. Since she was going to need a heart specialist, he handed it over to more experienced hands. Charlie calling the doctor named on the medical alert band that Rebecca had on had been a waste of precious time. The man had not seen her in over ten years. After calling around to other physicians in the area, they not only found her doctor, but he also gave them a long list of ailments that Rebecca was suffering from, as well as how she was doing nothing to take care of them. In addition to her congestive heart failure, she was a diabetic, had had several mini strokes, and had DVT in both her legs. Booker wasn't a doctor, but even he could understand the bad shape the elderly woman was in.

Rayne was on duty when they arrived. Charlie was taking her home to pick up Selma and Grandda—what they'd all been calling Mr. Oliver—and bring them back to the hospital. Booker was just sitting down for a long wait when not only his dad showed up, but the rest of the family as well. Booker asked his dad what was going on.

"We're here to donate blood. I heard from someone once that during every crisis there is a need. Not that this is a major one, but there isn't any reason we can't help out. Charlie and Rayne both are our family now, and we're going to help out." As it turned out they were in short supply of blood at the hospital, and were thrilled when the uncles and his father gathered together to make some calls about others coming in as well. Booker was getting tested for his blood when Charlie and the rest of them showed up.

"Are you going to assist on the surgery?" Both women said that while they were doctors, they didn't have the experience in assisting yet. "I guess I knew that. How is your grandda, Rayne? Is he doing all right?"

"He is. It's funny that—well, not funny ha-ha, but funny all the same—we were just talking about this very thing happening to Rebecca. She's been out of shape for some time. The medics said she weighed just under three hundred and sixty pounds when they brought her in this time. That's up twenty pounds since she'd been to the doctor before, Aunt Selma told us." Shaking her head, she looked at Charlie. "She was so calm when we went to get Grandda and Aunt Selma. I would have been freaking out."

"You *were* freaking out. One of us had to be calm." The two of them hugged. "It's all right. When I fall apart, you can calm me down when I do the same thing. Deal?"

Abby and the rest of the women showed up too. They handed out bottles of water to everyone, and also said that dinner was going to be brought in for them and the staff. Wats had told them the surgery could go on well into the evening. They were going to repair as much as they could of her heart, as that seemed to be what was giving her the most trouble for now.

"She's going to have to be put on an insulin pump. Also, a strict dietary plan. If she doesn't try and help herself, she won't be around for very much longer." Charlie asked about her legs. They had looked purplish when she'd been brought in. "We'll have a look at them, but at this point, since she coded twice in the ambulance on the way here, we're going to keep her heart going so we can work on the rest."

Charlie walked away a few minutes after they all gathered to wait it out, and Booker went to find her. He was still waiting on his blood to come back as clear—the place was a little overwhelmed with the uncles calling everyone to come in and donate. Charlie was sitting in one of the other waiting rooms staring out at the afternoon sun. He sat beside her and took her hand into his before speaking.

"Are you all right, honey?" Charlie nodded. "You look exhausted. Or is it worrying that has you looking so tired? I don't know your facial expressions well enough yet, so I'm only guessing."

"She was told no less than fifty times that she

needed to shed the weight, Selma told us on the way in. Two hundred pounds overweight, Booker. That's another whole person." He nodded. "She'd be in much better shape if she were to have shed just a hundred pounds. I'm not downing heavy people, but she has issues that pertain to her living, and getting the weight off would have given her a great many more years to be around. I just don't understand people. If you take the time to go to the doctor, why wouldn't you do what he tells you? Do they only go for the fun of it?"

"I don't know, honey. I really don't." When he was cleared to give blood, Booker went back to the little room they'd been using to give blood. Charlie started the IV for the staff and did a good job of it, he thought. "Did I tell you the medical examiner let Uncle Clayton know that there was nothing wrong with Eita's brain? She was just evil for the thrill of it. He's taking it better than I thought he would. At least he knows it wasn't something he could have gotten her treatment for." Charlie turned away when he spoke about his aunt. He let the subject go. She was very tender hearted today, he noticed. When she turned back, she had a bright yet forced smile on her face. He kissed her.

"I saw the posters your dad has been putting out." They both laughed. "I thought it was funny that he was going to run on the ticket of whatever they'd been promised by the sitting mayor, he was going to actually do. About your aunt, however—there are a great many evil people in the world. Just look at Phoenix and Fran. Those two were evil too, but didn't give two piles of crap about how anything they did affected anyone but them. I think at some point in their lives, they would have thought, perhaps, I'm a bad person and should change my ways. Maybe someday we can have a nice life without all the drama. But then, I guess it's too late for thinking like that so that my mom would still be around. She was murdered by a couple of grade a idiots."

"If Abby were here, she'd tell you it's not the drama we're going through, but the end result that we should be celebrating. Without your mom being murdered, as much as I hate to say this, I'd have never met you. The same with Aunt Holly being murdered. None of us would have been able to get to know our fathers on a much better level than it was. I thought Aunt Holly was the glue that held us all together, but I'm beginning to see we're all the glue that holds ourselves together." She just stared at him. "I'm not saying this right, am I?"

"You are. I was just thinking about the chain of events that brought me to you. And you're right. It had a great deal to do with the fact that you and the others are so honest and friendly. I mean, Mom being killed too. But you're kind to not just each other, but to everyone. My mom, she certainly loved all you guys. Especially North. She told me a few times that she thought he'd make a great sitting judge." Booker said he was just happy to have his own practice now. "Yes, now. And that will be good for him too. But I believe, now that I've gotten to know him better and with the support that he has, North would make a great judge. He's very knowledgeable, and has wonderful people skills."

He would too, Booker thought. When Charlie was called away, he sat there thinking about their lives since Aunt Holly had been murdered. No matter how he thought about it, had she not been killed and brought them all together, they—none of them— would be where they were today. He didn't even think Mars would be married to Abby, with a child on the way. Christ. It was true. Something had to happen, a murder in this case, to have brought them to be a family once again.

After he'd given his blood, he went to sit with the others. One at a time they'd get up to go and check on something, take their turn giving blood, or run for food or drinks, but none of them left the hospital for any longer than they had to.

At ten after ten that night, Wats came to talk to them. "The massive stroke Rebecca had while talking to us did a great deal more damage not just to her heart, but her body as well. With her weakened system and the weight she had put on, even with all the work we had been doing for her, I'm sorry, there was no saving her." James nodded and Selma held onto his hand. Rayne cried softly sitting next to them. James asked about donating her liver and such to help someone else. "I'm sorry. With her health issues, there is nothing to salvage to be used for someone else. I'm terribly sorry, sir."

"She never thought the doctors that told her to lose weight had a bit of sense. Rebecca was forever blaming them for the death of Robert." Booker asked Selma who Robert was. "Our brother. He would have been Rayne's grandfather."

Everyone looked at James. He laughed a little. "I'm actually her great grandfather. Rayne's father and grandfather, my grandson and son, were killed in a boating accident when Rayne was just a wee little thing. Her momma, a tiny little thing too, couldn't take raising Rayne up on her own, so she lit out when Rayne started grade school. Never looked back either." James looked at Rayne and smiled. "I've never regretted a day since then that she was left with us."

"I don't understand. How is it the doctors fault if he was killed in a boating accident?" James started laughing first, then Selma. Booker didn't know what had happened, but whatever it was, he was sure it was going to be funny. When Selma said she'd tell him, everyone gathered around to hear what she had to say.

"My brother was drunk and fell out of the boat. His son, also very drunk, tried to save him, but fell into the water trying to drag him into the boat. They both drowned. I know that's tragic, but honestly, it was going to be something like that with those two. If they both weren't drunk by the end of the afternoon, either they had run out of whiskey or they were ill. But they both drowned because they didn't remember they could swim." She snickered a little. "Rebecca blamed it on the doctor every time someone would bring up the two of them, because the doctor had told them they needed to get up off their asses and walk. Also, be one with nature and drink more fluids. They were doing just what their doctor told them to do when they died. Drinking while outside. She blamed the doctor for telling him he needed to get out more and to drink. I was never able to make her understand that was not what he meant, but she would never believe me."

Booker laughed first. Then the others joined them. It wasn't until they were joined by the surgeon that they were able to get it under control. He thought there was a special kind of place for people like Rebecca. Booker just wasn't sure where that would be — or if he ever wanted to visit there.

Arrangements were made for Rebecca to be taken to the funeral home. Wats helped James with the arrangements while he took care that Salma was taken home, as well as Rayne. She was taking it well, he thought. But then, all of them seemed to be. Rebecca had been a force for so long that he was sure they weren't sure how to react to her being gone.

Booker and his cousins were all a product of that kind of relief. Their mothers were gone, and he still found himself flinching when he did something he knew his mom wouldn't have approved of, looking around for her or one of her henchmen to take him to task. Booker wondered if he'd ever be able to get over that, and decided right then and there that he was going to. Even if he had to have a long talk with himself every day.

Chapter 3

Charlie was beginning to feel like a real doctor. She was, she knew that, but now she was making decisions as one, and feeling really good about them. It was for the people that came to her expecting her to have the right information to make them better. Also, even though she still did it on occasion, she didn't go to Wats to ask him every time she thought she had the right answer for someone she was seeing. At the end of a fairly busy day, she was in her office when Wats came in to see her.

"I have one more patient to see today, but I want to go home and play with the kids. I was wondering if I could persuade you to take it." She told him she'd gladly do that for him. "Thanks. I'll owe you. The patient is an elderly man, Mr. Stanley Tolliver. He comes in once a week for me to do his bloodwork for his blood thinners. He's usually within range, but he insists I do it weekly so he's not caught unawares. I think he's just lonely, and comes here for some conversation."

"I'll talk to him as long as he wants. Booker is working at the shop today with his dad. Also, there are a couple of things here I wanted to take care of. Did you know there are seven babies at the hospital that have nowhere to go after they're released? Seven of them. Sheesh. What the hell is going on?" Wats told her his opinion. "Okay, I guess I can see that. But it still doesn't make me feel any better about it. Not being able to afford another mouth to feed seems like someone isn't thinking all the way through the process. There are methods of not getting pregnant every time someone has sex."

He was still laughing when he left her. She, however, didn't see the humor in it. Seven little babies, through no fault of their own, were now going to be put into the system, and who knew what lay in store for their little lives from then on? As she finished up her paperwork on the children she'd gone to see for their physicals, she noticed that Mr. Tolliver hadn't come in yet. Going to the front to make sure he wasn't waiting on Wats, she asked Adilene, their nurse, if he'd called in.

"I was just about to give him a call to see what

was going on. Sometimes he has to wait on a ride from one of his grandchildren. Poor old thing. He nearly raised those grandchildren of his, and they have no more respect for him than they do a pile of poop in the yard. Let me give him a call." Charlie said that if he was waiting on a ride, she could go out there and see him. "Oh, that would be wonderful. Let me just have a talk with him. Hello?"

Putting it on speaker when Adilene looked about as distressed as she'd ever seen her, listening for several seconds, Charlie heard some shouting. Waiting for someone to actually speak to them, Charlie gathered up her things in anticipation of going out to his home. Adilene asked the person to repeat what they'd said.

"I said he's not going to be able to come in today, as he doesn't have any cash to give me for gasoline. The crazy old shit has already cashed his check and spent it all. I've look— Shut the fuck up, old man, before I shut you up. I've looked everywhere for it. I'm assuming he's spent it on shit." Adilene asked the person if the doctor could come out there. "I don't give a shit, but he's not going to pay extra for that shit to happen. Grandda hasn't got a pot to piss in as it is now. Christ, I don't know why he don't just die and get it over with." Then the line went dead.

"Call the police and have them go out with me,

Adilene. I don't know what the hell is going on out there, but you can bet I'm going to be taking care of it when I get there. So if I have to kill someone to get heads to roll, I'd rather have a witness on my side." She nodded as she picked up the phone again. "Also, let whoever of the family is around know that I'm headed out there. That way if his grandkids try something, at least they'll have some idea as to what is going on."

"You be careful." She said she would, and at the last minute tucked her weapon in her bag. There wasn't anyway she was going out there without some sort of protection. "I'm going to call that husband of yours too. Let him know where you're headed."

Charlie knew if she was still in the office when Adilene talked to Booker, he'd tell her not to go until she had some sort of backup. So hurrying out to her car, she was both happy and dismayed to find Josiah by her car. After telling him what was going on, he simply got into her car to go with her. Apparently she was taking him to the house, and she found she really was glad for the help. Laughing as she got into the car, she told him more of what was going on. Josiah pulled out his cell phone and called Clayton. He was nearby, Josiah told her.

"All righty then, an adventure. I hope one that ends well. We were out to see Mr. Tolliver just the other day, Clayton and I. We had a nice talk about what he was going to do with his land when he passes. Not leaving it to his family was high on his list." She told him what she'd heard over the phone. "That sounds like them. There's Clayton now. We'll take him with us. He called Booker to let him know we're with you too."

Charlie wasn't sure what was going to happen when she got out there, but she was now glad for the company of not just the family, but a family full of attorneys. The police, Officer Carson Dutch, showed up just as she and the other two men were getting out of the car. Charlie walked up to the house, calling for Mr. Tolliver as soon as she was on the porch. Every one of her backup was literally right on her heels.

She was let in by a man she'd never met before. Asking after Mr. Tolliver, he told her his name was Ben and that he was his oldest grandson. Also that he was there to make sure she didn't give him anything. She asked him what he thought she was going to give him.

"A message. I don't know, bitch. I came here to get his check, and he tells me it arrived early and he cashed it to pay bills. He's a stubborn old horse's ass when he gets something into his head." Charlie asked where he was. "In the kitchen. I didn't do anything to

him, no matter what he tells you. He's touched in the
head is what's wrong with him. I'm going to see about
having him put away while I'm here this time."

"Really? Well that'll suck for you, since the
nursing home will get his checks from now on." The
man asked Clayton if that was true. "Why would I
have a reason to lie to you? Of course they'll take it.
Who do you think would pay for it if they didn't take
it?"

"Then he'll stay right where he is. You'd not
believe the shit I have to go through to get a little
money from him every fucking month. You'd think
by now he'd know to just fork it over." Charlie went
into the kitchen with Ben right behind her. She could
hear Clayton talking about how the money was
supposed to support his grandda and not him, but it
wasn't anything Ben wanted to hear apparently, and
he followed her. "I didn't do shit to him. You tell them
that, Grandda. I didn't hurt you a bit."

Mr. Tolliver was sitting on the only piece of
furniture that wasn't busted up. The counters were
emptied because everything that had been on them
was also all over the floor and smashed up. The table
looked as if someone had landed on it, and there was
blood all over the place. Saying his name quietly, Mr.
Tolliver looked up at her.

Both his eyes were nearly swollen shut. She thought his nose was broken, and his upper lip was split open. With his left ear bleeding, she was sure he was going to have head injuries. After checking his wrist that Mr. Tolliver was holding in his other hand, she determined it was broken. Quickly checking the rest of him, just a preliminary examination, she asked him what he wanted to do.

"I want to go to the hospital, young lady." She nodded and told him she thought that might be a good idea. Ben said no. "I hurt bad. He done it too. Ben beat me to snot because I didn't have my money here waiting on him. I want to press charges. You come here with the police, I'm going to surely use them to keep my house and myself safe from his crap."

Ben lunged at Mr. Tolliver. Charlie pushed him over as he was leaning over the elderly man and he hit the floor hard. Good, she thought. She might well pay for it later if he got out, but for now she'd keep her patient safe.

Carson pulled Ben up from the floor and into the living room, and read him his rights. Having Josiah call for an ambulance, she did a more thorough check of Mr. Tolliver's head wound. It was going to require stitches for sure, but she also wanted to make sure as to what had caused the wound.

"He hit me with the chair there. Busted it all up. Then while I was down there begging for him to stop, he goes and kicks me. Is Wats coming along?" She said she was his partner, but if he wanted him, she'd make sure he was at the hospital when they arrived. "I'd like that a bit. Not that I don't think you're a good doctor or anything, miss. But I have me a pain in my private parts that I'd not show a pretty little thing like you."

"Did he kick you there, Mr. Tolliver?" He said he had stomped on him. "You leave it to me. I'll call Wats right now and have him meet us there."

Mr. Tolliver wasn't able to walk on his own. The medics were, however, able to lift him up, chair and all that he was sitting on, and put him into the ambulance. Charlie wanted to hunt down Ben and tear him a new ass. She thought if he was related to her, she'd take Mr. Tolliver to her home and take good care of the poor man.

As soon as they arrived at the hospital, Wats was there waiting on them. Mr. Tolliver broke down, telling Wats how sorry he was to have called him in. As soon as he was taken to a room, still in the chair, he was given something for pain and when he was out, put onto a gurney. The poor man still cried out in pain when he was laid down.

It took them both two hours to stitch Mr. Tolliver

up. After the X-rays showed he had a concussion and a brain bruise, he was set up with pain medication, as well as having his arm set and his groin taken care of. Wats said that even him being a doctor didn't prepare him for what the grandson had done to his grandda.

"His genital area is all right, but he certainly bruised the inside of his thighs to the point I think he meant to really break his legs. As it is, he's going to have to be on a catheter for a few days. At least until the swelling goes down." Wats shook his head as he continued. "No one should have to suffer like that after working all their life to get benefits coming to them, only to have some shit take them from them."

"Someone should do the same to him. All over a check that didn't belong to the kid in the first place. I tell you, Wats, every day I have less and less confidence in people doing the right thing by their elders. Every single day." Charlie had lost that confidence the day her mom had been murdered, but didn't bring it up to Wats. He was upset enough.

"I'm going to have him go into a nursing home after he leaves here, only to have him get the care he needs. Which reminds me. I know Tolliver has a grandson out there that does come to visit him and sends him money every month. I'll look into contacting him somehow. I wonder if Ben knew about this other kid. I only happened on the information a few months ago when I was talking to him about family."

"He would have said something, I'm sure. The fucking bastard." They both laughed, which was what she'd been going for. "He's a sweet old man. I hate that he's been treated this way."

Booker joined them after they had everything settled, and they brought him up to date on what they'd been talking about concerning North.

"My dad is going to help him with some things that will keep him safe. The house that Mr. Tolliver is living in is part of what Mars owns. Perhaps we can do him a little better and put him in a condo for the duration of his life. I know I'd feel better if he was living where someone could see him daily." She asked Booker if Ben was going to be in jail all that long. "It will depend on what the courts have to say about his treatment of his grandfather. You and I might have to talk to him if he needs convincing, but I have no way of knowing what this new judge will say. He won't even be here until Wednesday if there is a need for him."

"North should take the job. I've said this before, but I know my mom thought he'd make a great replacement for when she retired." Wats said he would need convincing too. "Perhaps I can talk him into it. I have some of the notebooks my mom left me that talk about him taking her place. It was a dream of hers to work with North as a judge. She had a great deal of respect for him."

"Talk to him. I think he'd do a great job as judge myself, especially with our uncles and his dad in his corner. I've heard they're doing a good job of making sure their clients are happy after their trial." Charlie said she'd heard that as well. "They seem to enjoy working together as well. Uncle Clayton will make a fantastic mayor too."

After making sure Mr. Tolliver was going to be in good hands, the two of them left. Wats made his way to his house — holding the babies, he said, was the best stress reliever he'd ever encountered. As she made her way to her car, Charlie talked to Booker about what was going on. He asked her if she was going to talk to North soon.

"Why? Do you know something I don't?" He shrugged. "That's not an answer, buster. What is going on? Something I need to know about before I go and convince him that he needs to take this job so people get justice from their troubles?"

"It's just that I don't think he's any happier at what's going on with the new judge working this area into his schedule than you are. I know I'm not. Every time I need to go by the courthouse to file something, like a patent, or even something I've purchased, like land, I have to wait. Not as long as a court hearing or showing, but it is important for me to follow the rules." She said she could see that. "Also, you might not know this, but you should talk to Mars. He's got some ideas on how to convince North to take the job. Mostly it's to do with the seven babies in the hospital now that you were talking about earlier. No one can take them into their care or even adopt them until they're released by the judge. It's a pain in the ass for anyone wanting to adopt them. Also, there aren't any background checks going on when needed. Your mom took care of all of that for the town."

"I need to talk to him. I want us to have a staff, and I never thought of that being the reason behind it taking so long to happen. All we have now is a cook and a sometimes chauffeur." Charlie looked up at Booker. "Well, are you going with me or not? I'm going to do it right now, and if you want to be his witness when I have to start knocking him around, now would be the time to go with me."

"I'll be your witness in this. And it will be my pleasure to knock him around should he need it as well." Booker got into the car with her and kissed her quickly on the mouth. "This is going to be the perfect ending to my day. Also, before I forget to tell you, the house is finished. So is Mars and Abby's home. They're going to have us all over for dinner in a couple of days to celebrate."

"I'd like that. And I'm thrilled beyond words to have our home finished up. I got sick of trying to find which room they were working on so I could go to the other end of the hall, only to be told they had equipment in there that they needed." He laughed as she backed out of the parking lot. "I love you, Booker. So very much."

"And I love you, Charlie. More than words could convey. Let's go and have some fun with North, go home, then make love." She told him that was her thinking too. "Also, something else I forgot to tell you, we're having company tomorrow night. They're coming to the house to look over my plans for the two games I have in the works. I'm very excited to be able to do this on my own for a change. Not having someone standing over my shoulder making me work at their pace has made it so I can work on whatever I want, whenever I want. It's very liberating."

North was home when they arrived. He was just getting ready to start on some burgers they were grilling out, and invited them to join them. She wondered if he'd be so nice as to invite them again when he figured out what they were really there for. As it was, when Amy joined them after a photo shoot at her new building, they were ready to do battle. If necessary.

~*~

North wasn't sure what his family was there for, but he was glad to have Booker out on the deck with him. Standing there, thinking about his day, he turned to his cousin to tell him where his mind had been for the last several days. Mostly his job.

"I'm thinking of running for the judge position for this county." Patting Booker on the back when he started coughing hard, he asked him what had happened. "Christ, if you think it's a bad idea, I might have to rethink my plans."

"It's not that." Booker told him he was all right now. "That's the reason we've come by. To convince you that you need to take the position. Christ, Charlie is going to be so disappointed that she can't knock you around."

"I'm not sure how I should be feeling about that. Really?" They both laughed. "I've been thinking about all the things I could be doing that aren't getting done now. I don't care for the judge either. She was a bit of a bastard the two times I've had to talk to her. Like just because she made it all the way to being a judge she somehow is so much better than those around her. Bitch. As if I have nothing else to do but to chase her down for information to set up a trial. The last straw was the other night when I called her office, telling them how important it was that I get a call back as soon as possible, and she didn't bother. Told me her time was her own, and if I thought I could do a better job then I was to take the job myself. I decided I would."

At dinner, adding more food to the grill when Abby and Mars showed up, they talked about the requirements he'd have to have under his belt before he could even put it on the ballot. It was Mars that spoke up about that.

"I've looked into it. You can take the county seat over now as a temporary judge. Since we're a fairly big area here with a population count that is decent, you can apply to be put in the position by a letter of recommendation from the state. I've already talked to someone about that." Mars handed North a thick envelope. "Mom had some pretty amazing contacts, and after your dad and the others called and talked to the man, you have the seat now. All you need to do is be sworn in and you'll be official. So you know, that's going to happen in the morning at the courthouse. I don't like having to wait on every little thing I need done."

If North was surprised by what was happening and the speed at which it was, he didn't act like it. Instead, he looked over the paperwork, signed his name where the tabs were, and finished off his burger. No one said a word for several seconds until Amy started laughing.

"Remind me to never tell you guys I'm impatient for something. I don't think the postal service will stand a chance with you guys once you set your mind to something." They all laughed and agreed with Amy. "I also, while the getting things done mood is still going on, have decided to put in my own darkroom. I have one now, but this one will be larger and able to handle larger photos than I can print now. I'm so excited I could bust."

"You need us to get you any of the equipment coming in?" Booker kissed Charlie when she offered. "The hospital is also getting new equipment in, thanks to a generous donation from an anonymous doner. Thank you, Mars and Abby. The new wing for the children's cancer ward is going to be state of the art. And the way things are working there, I have an idea there will be more improvement as the days go on."

As they were cleaning up the small mess they'd made, North was telling them about his day. How at some point the police had come to him about staffing.

Booker hadn't even been aware they needed someone in place to take on that sort of project.

"I didn't either. But as I began to look at the things I can do as a sitting judge, temporary or not, I realized a lot of things aren't happening that should have been taken care of years ago. One of them is the promises that Mayor Billings didn't take care of when he was put into office. Also, and this one surprised me the most, Billings hasn't had anyone run against him since he was put in office fourteen years ago. I'm going to have to talk to my dad about that. See if he's used any bullying tactics against him." Booker asked him what else he'd been able to find. "The sidewalks were paid for several years ago. The contract was given to the lowest bidder, of course, but nothing has been done. Every time I try to find the company that was supposed to have been in charge of it, I hit a dead end. Like the company never existed."

"You think Billings pocketed the money?" North didn't answer him yes or no, but the look on his face told volumes. "Do I want to guess where the money has gone?"

"It's not been used, that much I do know. The money had been earmarked for Jackson's construction, and they're the only company that can pick the money up. I'm thinking Billings hadn't thought it all the way through, and he can't get to the money either." That made him laugh. "Whoever set it up for him put it in an interest bearing account, and the money isn't doing that well, but it's more than what was put in the account. Also, the water treatment plant should have been inspected years ago, and yearly since then. There are no records of anyone doing that either."

"It sounds to me like you should take this job for the sole reason of getting us clean water. Or would that be the mayor?" North told him what he'd been able to figure out. "All right. I guess that makes more sense. Since we know Lorrinda wouldn't have been able to let that go, we'll have to look through her books to see what she was thinking about it. And see what we can find out about anything else the sitting mayor is doing."

North called his dad, and he said he'd be over soon. He and Aiden were hanging out, working on a speech. There was going to be a town hall meeting on Wednesday that his dad had called. It was going to be epic, Booker thought, and decided to call a few people he knew to see if he could get some state coverage of it. It would go a long way in helping North with his new job to have a lot of things brought to the surface with the little town.

"The best I can tell, of the fifty-one things he

promised to have finished by the first year of his term, none of them have been started. The sidewalk issue has become bad, so bad I'm thinking even with the money in the bank now, it's not going to cover the costs of it. Also, and this isn't really anything I'm surprised by, but the hospital is behind on their property taxes. I wasn't even aware they had to pay any. But I'm looking into that too." Uncle Clayton tossed the papers on the table, frustrated. They'd been going over things since they'd arrived an hour ago. His uncle continued as he sat down, rubbing his hand over his face. "There was a time when we said the land could be used for the purpose of having a place for the hospital. But for the life of me, I can't figure out where that ran out."

"Abby and I own the property being used. I think it's also a part of the nursing home that sits beside it. If you can give me a minute, I can make a couple of calls and find out what is going on there." Mars left the room to make his calls.

"Something else that has been bothering me. And it might just be that I've watched too many of those murder shows at night where money is the root of all evil, but where is the money going for the taxes? I don't just mean the hospital, but the other places around town as well." It was then that his dad picked up the papers his brother had tossed down. After thumbing through them quickly, he looked around the table. "I mean, I can't believe the hospital is behind on taxes, much less the rest of the city. There is also some missing money that should have been able to keep the water department in new trucks every four years, as well as the school yards being repaved and the equipment upgraded. I'm not saying he stole it all, but just explain to me where it could be." Mars joined them. If his face was any indication, he didn't know anything more than they did. "What do you know, Mars, son?"

"The hospital doesn't pay any taxes until such time as they are no longer a viable entity. I have an idea what that means—they have to be a hospital. There are things in here too that I wonder why my mom didn't take care of. Like when the building is in need of repair, as well as adding new wings, they're able to borrow the money directly from Adobe Well at no or very little interest. If they are unable to secure the loan, our company would help with the paying off of the loan." Mars looked around the room. "The entire hospital could use an upgrade if you were to ask me. And I know for a fact that the outside of the building could use a new paint job and some trees replanted. Mom didn't care for trees in the lot, she told me that would be just inviting trouble, but the outside of the parking lot needs some major overhauling."

Booker took notes that he was going to check into. The taxes the hospital was supposed to have been behind on were in the millions of dollars. While he wasn't sure Billings had anything to do with them thinking the hospital needed to be paying, Booker was sure he had some sort of hand in the dealings. Booker voiced his concerns.

"He does." They all turned to Charlie when she spoke up. "Mom kept notes on all sorts of things, as you know. There is a notation in one of her books that tells how Billings was sniffing around about how the hospital wasn't making any profit, and that it would need to close up soon. After she spoke to him — more like cornered Billings and screamed at him — he confessed that he was going to buy the property for a song, then sell it off to get a for profit only hospital in. I'm not sure what that means, but it can't be good for the community."

"It pretty much means the board or owner of the hospital can charge as much as they want for any kind of treatment and get away with it." Clayton sat down as he continued. "I wonder if any of the previous board members knew this was going to be in the works. If so, it explains a great deal about how they wanted to keep themselves around. To share in all the profits."

"They can't do that." Mars handed the paperwork off to North. "If they change the nonprofit for a profit one, then I cannot only take the land the hospital sits on, but Abby and I would own every improvement they've ever made. Such as the hospital and equipment in it."

"Do you care if I mention that, Mars? I'd not say your name, of course, but I can talk about it at the meeting tomorrow. I'm sure Billings is going to try and bring that up in a better light than we've been able to reason out."

"Go ahead. Now some of the conversations going on at the pharmacy are starting to fall into place. One of my customers was saying that if the hospital were to go to profit only, everyone would be making a little off the services. She thought it would be more than enough to take care of the slight rise in cost of services. I doubt very much that Billings will share with the town, anymore than he will anything else he has his hand in." Booker wrote that down too for Clayton. "Also, Uncle Clayton, I've been meaning to ask you if you've had any trouble with Billings. I've heard he has been threatening anyone that dares to run against him for a great many years. I wouldn't put it past him to do the same to you."

"He's been bullying me around, sure. But I

expected that." Uncle Clayton paused a moment. "Now that I think on it, it wasn't bullying, but he was downright threatening me. Like telling me the town was going to be pissy about the fact my wife had been such a bully. And that I was related to the whore. Holy Christ. You think he was talking about my sister?"

"I'd say that's a fair bet." No one said anything more. Booker stood up, gathering the attention of everyone in the room. "This meeting tomorrow. I think we should all go there and voice our own concerns about Billings. Not just the money, but the threats I've heard myself around town that he's putting out there against everyone."

"Good idea."

When they left the house, simply driving across the yard to his own home, he decided he was going to get with North to see if he could get a nice driveway put in between their homes. It would be nice on nights like this one to not have to travel twice the distance when it wasn't necessary. Yes, he thought, they had a great deal to talk about starting tomorrow.

Chapter 4

Charlie had her notes, along with the others, all put into a file. There were tabs on them too, showing whatever was brought up at the meeting so she only had to pull it from the file and hand it out. Everyone, all the Wilkersons, had their own notes as well. Things they were going to bring up.

"Are you ready, honey?" She loved Clayton and the rest of the uncles. Josiah had been hanging around them more and more daily, and she hoped it was because he was thinking of moving in with them. The house, she had told him, was so big he could come and go as he pleased, as well as be nearby when they needed to get a hug. She'd been getting used to the bear like hugs all the men gave. "This is going to be so much fun. I hope no one tries to pull out a gun or something. I'd surely hate to have myself wounded from all this."

Since she wasn't sure if he was being serious or not, she laughed when he did. There were a lot of strange thinking people around. To her, they were all strange, but she'd been changing her mind a little at a time about most people. Telling him she was as ready as she'd ever be, the meeting was called to order.

They'd had to use the large school gymnasium to have the meeting. There had been way too many people showing up at the courthouse, where the talk or whatever it was called was supposed to have been held. She was glad to see the townspeople were taking an interest in this meeting. Hopefully they'd have a bit more answers to some of the questions that had come up last evening.

Since Clayton had called the meeting, Billings was the first to talk. When he started out laughing, no one in the room joined him. It wasn't until Ms. Milner stood up that the room hushed even more. Teddy was standing right beside her.

"I was wondering why you've not done a darned thing you promised us you'd do when your bottom was put into office all those years ago. I'm not accusing you of cheating, but I bet if someone would have a look at it, there were a mite more votes for you than there are people in three counties around here. Are you ever going to get off that fat duff of yours and do anything?" Billings started to laugh again, but it was forced. Before he could speak, Ms. Milner spoke again. "I don't think there is a thing funny about any of this. I have me a list here that tells all the things promised to us as a town that you've not done one thing of. Starting with the sidewalks. Then there is the school grounds that need to be fixed up. Also, the cemetery that needs to have a good—" Billings cut her off and told her he was working on them. "No you're not, you lying fat tub of lard. And don't you dare cut me off again. I'm an old woman, and I deserve respect. I'm thinking you don't know the meaning of that word, so let me tell you. You honor those that know a darn site better than you do. Now sit down and shut up whilst I go over my own grievances about you."

Charlie watched the people around the town stand up one at a time, always deferring to Ms. Milner before they spoke. Not only did someone touch on everything on the Wilkerson's list, but they were also able to bring up a great deal more things that none of them had been aware of. When Billings turned to the doorway, he was sweating like the pig he'd been called.

"Mr. Anderson. Surely you have something to say that is nicer than all these people have been saying." Anderson stood up and stood there, staring at first Clayton, then back at Billings. "You do have some words to say about me. I'm sure of it."

"I thought I did. I truly did. Even after seeing something the other day that made me realize you're just as much a shit—pardon me, Miss Milner—but you're just as much a poop-head as these people here are saying about you. Worse, I think." Putting his hand into the bib part of his coveralls, Anderson rocked on his heels back and forth for several seconds before he began to speak again. "Four days ago I was working in my yard when I heard the worst caterwauling I've ever heard. Looked up in time to see that Pincher boy sitting on the sidewalk with his arm bleeding, like he was gonna be meeting his maker soon. Then, just like them movies my grandkiddies like to watch, Mr. Wesley and Doc Wats there scooped him up and took off running to the clinic with him. They must have been out painting the town, as my own grannie used to say, on account'a them being dressed to the nines and all. But they didn't care a wit for the blood staining them suits they had on. Nor the dirt that got on their knees when they were helping the young lad out. Doc there, he pulled off that tie of his—I'm betting it cost more than my groceries for a week—he put that tie right around that little boy's arm as they were walking and talking to him. Couldn't have given my heart a better jolt than to see them doing that."

"I'm sure any one of us would have—" Mr. Anderson said he wasn't nearly finished. And like Ms. Milner, he didn't appreciate being interrupted. "I'm sorry. Do go on. But I do want to point out that I'd have done the same thing."

"If'n you had fixed up the sidewalk in the first place, like you went and promised us nearly two decades ago, then that boy would be out playing in his yard, not all cooped up like a brooding hen waiting on her chicks to hatch." Billings wiped his forehead again. "Then you know what happened? That Mr. Clayton there, he and a couple of them nephews of his come along, without no fanfare either, and not only fixed up the broken sidewalk, but had a crew come out the next afternoon and fixed up the entire sidewalk right then and there." Anderson looked at Clayton. "He paid me fifty dollars to come here and badmouth you, Mr. Clayton. I worked at it real hard on trying to find one thing to say about you that wasn't what my grannie would call complimentary toward you. She was funny about using them big words. All I could think about was that boy and the sidewalk. You go on now and be the mayor if you wouldn't mind. I know I'd like to have someone in that building that does what he says, even if there ain't no crew of television people standing there with a film recorder in their face."

No one said anything for several minutes. Then Billings simply gathered up his things and turned to Clayton. Charlie stood up, with the rest of the senior Wilkersons there for support, and waited to see what the man was going to do next. Booker, along with his cousins, came up from the seated area and stood beside him. It wasn't going to end well if Billings even farted right now.

"We'll see who the better man is, won't we, Clayton?" Clayton smiled and said he already had a good idea who that better man was. "You think you're all high and mighty, don't you? Thinking because you have all kinds of money, you can just come in and take a person's livelihood from them. Well, I'm not worried about you. You're shit for all I care about you running against me."

"I guess we'll find out in about two weeks, now won't we?" Billings looked around the room at all of the family that had come out to support Clayton. "Since you brought up livelihood, Billings, where is the money for the water department improvements? Or the school yard money? Then there is the taxes that are said to be owed on the hospital. I know for a fact there wouldn't be any back taxes on the place. Are you perhaps trying to sabotage the hospital so you can make it a for-profit place?"

"Who told you?" He seemed to realize he had given himself away, and began to backtrack on what he'd said. "I don't have any idea what you're talking about. You're just blowing shit out of your ass now so you can win. Well, I'm going to win this election hands down. Just as I did every other time."

"Voter fraud is against the law, did you know that?" Billings paled but didn't speak. It was then that Clayton seemed to understand the room had gone silent. Pointing to her collar with a huge smile on her face, Charlieju09 pointed out that he was still wearing a live mike. As was Billings. Clayton smiled back at her. "Also, you should be aware that the FBI is looking into how so many people voted for you. With the counting of both yours and your opponent's votes, that was about ten percent more than the county seat has in the way of residents. Would you have any idea how that came about?"

"You're a liar. You're no better than the stupid people that live here. And don't think everyone in this town doesn't know what sort of person you were married to either. Christ, the things I could tell people about that she and those other bitches had—"

If Charlie hadn't been looking at Clayton when he moved, she wouldn't have believed it. Clayton didn't even hesitate in doubling up his fist and slamming it into Billings's face. The man went tumbling back and fell on his ass, much to the amusement of everyone still seated.

When he was helped to his feet, of course Billings had to threaten Clayton for what he'd done. Everyone knew the Wilkerson men hadn't been upset at the deaths of their wives. It was, to her anyway, doubtful that anyone in the entire state had been bothered overly much by their deaths. However, as Clayton explained, it was a matter of honor that he had to hit Billings.

"It's all right if I talk about my deceased wife the way you just did. Fine if my family hated her as much as I did. However, there isn't any reason for me to accept your mouth running about things that don't concern you. And the death of my wife, or any of the other wives, is none of your business. And I'd appreciate it if you were to remember that from now on." Billings was still running his mouth when he left the school. Clayton turned to the people still in the room with him. "I'm sorry about that, folks. It bothers me to no end the things that spew from people's mouths that doesn't concern them. However, if you have any questions about what my plans are for the town, you can go ahead and ask me."

Never referring to the notes, Clayton or one of

the others answered questions. Mostly it was to do with the larger projects he had already gotten a start on. There was some talk about the hospital staying the way it was, and Mars was able to answer everything pertaining to the contract about that. He didn't mention that he owned the land the hospital was on, but made it sound as if whoever did, this was what he knew they'd say about it.

When the meeting was finished up, nearly nine that night, a great many of the townspeople were still in attendance. Ms. Milner and Teddy had left, as they were needing to get home before dark. There were a lot of people asking Clayton if they could be a part of what he might have going on now. That was when the activity center/nursing home was brought up.

~*~

Booker walked around the inside of the building. He wasn't new to seeing worn down buildings, but this one would have been the worst if he'd had to scale it with the others. Even the outside of it was in much better shape than the inside. He was just walking out of one of the unused rooms when Charlie caught up with him.

"If I had a dog I'd not let it live here." He agreed with her. "The rooms are much too small for anyone not to be claustrophobic. There isn't any place for people to go out in the yard should someone like to have some activities out there."

"The kitchen is too small as well. It also doubles as a rec room when it's needed. The piano hasn't been touched in decades, so it's not just out of tune, but it also has most of the keys missing." She laughed when he said he'd played "Mary had a Little Lamb" on it. "And this is the real kicker. There isn't any working air conditioner. As in nowhere in this building, including the few rooms that are being used, has any way of cooling them off in the summer months. The furnace, I was told, has its own set of troubles. It hasn't worked well in over twenty years. Why the hell hasn't anyone said anything about this before now?"

"I haven't any idea. However, your uncles are going over all the paperwork taken from the mayor's office that the FBI is finished with. With Billings being arrested last night for trying to flee the country, Clayton has moved in to help out as much as he can. They're very impressed, Amy told me, on how your family has been taking over the more serious projects." She looked around the room they were in. "The wall paper in here makes me sick. I wonder if that was the plan? Who the heck thought that pink wallpaper with green paisley was a good idea?"

"I don't know, but if you don't move too quickly

it's not so bad." Booker pulled Charlie into his arms. "I missed you being in our bed when I woke up this morning. I know you had to be on call, but it was lonely there without you."

"You and I have had sex ten times a day since we've met. That doesn't include the quickies we've had in each room of the house. Last night on the way home from the high school we had sex again against a tree that was out in the open of anyone that would shine their lights in our direction. Maybe I was trying to escape. Did you ever think of that?"

He pretended to think about it, then grinned. "Nah, you love it. I love to hear you screaming out my name. And holy Christ, when you come down my throat, I nearly can't make it to be inside of you, it drives me that much over the edge." She smacked him. "I was only talking about how cold your side of the bed was when I woke up. Nothing to do with sex."

"Sure it wasn't." He was still laughing at her expression as they finished out the tour of the building. "I'm thinking there is just so much here to repair that it would be cheaper just to start over. While I know that any one of us could afford to have a nice big building put in its place, Dad said he wasn't keen on doing that, for the simple reason that it would set a precedent on having us put in new buildings for every little thing."

"He told me the same thing. Even Mars, who would help anyone that asked, isn't going to pony up the money for a new one. He said he was dealing with enough about the other things his mom owned in town. Did you know Mars owns the land the courthouse sits on? It had been handed down to him from his mother, who had been given it by a great-something grandma from when the town first started out." Booker said he did know that, as Mars had told him. "I wonder what Billings would have said to him had he known who the owner was of the hospital land. Mr. Montgomery told me the man was bitching about how — Booker, is that a snake?"

It was indeed a snake. And since he wasn't up on his snake knowledge, he and Charlie backed out of the room and closed the door. Pulling out his cell, he opened the door enough to get a picture of the creature before closing it again. He hated snakes with a passion.

"I'm calling my dad. Also anyone else that knows how the hell a snake might have gotten it's slimy self—"

"Snakes aren't slimy, you know?" They both turned and looked at the little boy in the wheelchair behind them. "Some have a texture, but they're not slimy at all. Cool and dry. That's what they are. Cool and dry."

"Do you know this one?" The little boy took the phone from him and nodded before handing it back. "Is it one of yours then? I mean, how else would it have gotten in here other than being brought in?"

"It's not mine. We're not allowed to have pets. Not that I'd be able to play with one anyway. But it gets in from the broken window in the kitchen. Rats too. However, he usually takes care of that problem if he sees them. Are you visiting someone?" Booker let Charlie tell him why they were there. "Inspecting this place, are you? Well, have you seen the lower levels? I used to go there all the time when I was younger and the elevator worked. Since it doesn't, I have to take the stairs, and those are slippery."

Charlie laughed, but all Booker could wrap his head around was the fact that this kid was here when snakes could get in. Letting Robbie Harley, the kid's name, show them around, Booker looked at things from the angle of a person stuck in a wheelchair, and how they might be getting around with all the things wrong with this place. He was glad Charlie asked to see his room.

"It's not big enough for all three of us to go in at once when I'm in my chair. So you guys go on in and I'll tell you anything you want to know." True to his word, Robbie stayed outside the room while the two of them entered. "I got some of the others that stay here to help me paint the walls. They didn't do a very good job, but it was better than what I had before. At least this way I can pretend I have a view. Mrs. Marple painted the flowers. She passed away a few years ago."

"How long have you been here, Robbie?" Booker didn't know why he had asked him that. It was rude for one thing, and it was none of his business. He continued to look at the "window" that had been painted on the wall, with the most colorful flowers he'd ever seen there as well. When he turned back, Robbie was smiling at him. "You have a wonderfully small room."

It was too. There was no equipment to get Robbie in and out of his bed, so he could only assume he had to do it himself. There wasn't enough room for the bed and single broken down dresser, much less anything else a boy would want. When the door was shut behind them, Robbie finally answered.

"A long time. When I was a baby, I guess they said I was ten months old, my dad and mom had a car accident and were both killed. Since no one wanted a cripple and there wasn't any money, I was stuck here. At first it wasn't so bad. Not with the others living here too. But as they die off I don't get to have as many friends to talk to." Charlie said she was sorry. "I used to be too, Ms. W. But since there isn't anything I can do about it, I just try hard to look on the bright side. At least I can get around. That's more than my parents can do."

It was a defense joke. Booker had used it a million times in ensuring himself that what his mother did was nothing to him. Instead of dealing with whatever had happened, he'd make a joke. Mostly to put himself in a bad light. Now that he was older, he could see it as an open wound on others, just as Aunt Holly had seen on him.

Getting down to Robbie's level, he stared at the boy. There was brilliance there. Sadness too, he could see. Booker put out his hand, and when Robby took it into his, he could feel the slight trembling of someone that wasn't just unsure of themselves, but what someone was going to do to them.

"You can't stay here. You understand that, don't you?" Robbie nodded, then looked away. He asked if he was going to have the place condemned. "Yes. We'll have to after seeing this place. Even if you weren't confined to a wheelchair, you have to know how dangerous it is for you to be here without help. When was the last time you were able to take a full shower? Or even to have someone help you with your laundry? I have to think it's been a while."

"Months. After Mr. Montgomery passed on. He didn't mind helping me, but can't no more." Tears flowed down Robbie's cheeks, and Booker asked him what he'd like to do. "I don't know what you mean. I guess they'll put me in one of those homes the doctor here tells me about all the time. She said I'd get better care, but I'd have to put up with sexual deviants."

"Who would say that to a kid?" Robbie told Charlie he didn't remember her name, but Booker had a feeling that not only did he know her name, but had a phone number for her as well. "You can bet I'm going to be looking into this, Robbie. There wasn't any reason whatsoever that anyone should say that to a child. You're coming home with us. Right now. I'll pack your things that you'll need for tonight, then tomorrow we'll figure out the rest. I can't believe some people. And she calls herself a doctor. Why, if she were here right now, I'd show her what a…well, I don't know how to finish that. So I won't."

The door shut behind Charlie as she went into Robbie's room. He could still hear her talking to herself, but not what she was saying anymore. Laughing, he looked down at Robbie when he looked up at him.

"She sure does seem mad. Did I do that?" Booker told him in a way, but a good one. "I don't know how that's possible. Being mad isn't good anyway you cut it. Am I really going home with you tonight?"

"Yes. My family would kick my butt if I even thought of leaving you here to fend for yourself. Not to mention, Charlie." Booker walked alongside of Robbie until they came to a bench. Booker was a big man and didn't chance sitting on the thing. "If you don't want to go home with us, I'm sure Charlie would stay here with you. But I'd not expect her to be any less upset about you being talked to that way. Do you know the doctor?"

"Yes, but I'm not going to tell her." Laughing again with the young man, Charlie came out of the room with some clothing in her hands. No luggage, but just an armful of clothing. "You got everything I own? I guess we won't have to come back then, huh?"

That tore at his heart more than he thought it would have. Everything Robbie owned didn't even cover both of Charlie's arms when she brought it to them. As they made their way out to the truck to take him home, he remembered they were having dinner with his dad tonight. Noticing the shape of his chair didn't help his heart, but he told Robbie where they were going.

"Really? I've never been out to eat before. And the pizza we would have here sometimes wasn't fit to eat, Mr. Montgomery told me all the time. It was all right, but a little greasy. What will your dad say about you bringing a crippled up kid with you?"

He answered him before he could even think about his words, or how many times Robbie had been called a cripple.

"I don't know what he'll say, but we'll ask him when one shows up. By the way, you're not crippled. Not even close. You're brave, strong, and resilient. I don't even know ten people I could say that about. My dad being one of them." Booker put the wheelchair in the back end. "Tomorrow we'll look into what has to be done for you to come and stay with us. You can sort of try us on too. All right?"

"Just like that. You're going to take me home with you? What if you change your mind about me staying overnight? You gonna bring me back here? I won't care so much, but you'll have to remember to do it before ten. They lock all the doors then, so no one can get in or out of here after that." Booker said he wanted to adopt him, not just take him home for a visit. Robbie looked at Charlie, who was nodding too. "You people are weird. I like you, don't get me wrong, but you're way weird. All right. I'll try you on. But if you have to bring me back here, please, oh please don't just leave me. I'd like something to bring back with me. You see, I've not only not been out to eat before, but I've never been out of here at all. Not even to the sidewalk because of the stairs."

"We're not going to be taking you back to anyplace, young man. Now. Listen to your dad and get buckled in and I'll check it out." Nodding once, Booker made sure the buckle was tight enough while Charlie said she forgot her purse. She didn't carry one as far as he knew.

"She gonna be all right, Booker?" He said she was emotional and happy. "Yeah? She sure has a funny way of showing it. I didn't know someone who cried when they were happy before."

"Women do all kinds of strange things. Cry when they're happy. Cry when they're powerfully upset. They'll tell you off right to your face, then have a good cry about that too." Robbie asked him why he'd want to be around someone like that all the time. "Because I love her. And learning to tell the difference between her happy cries and her sad ones is something I'm hoping to understand someday. I want her to be happy all the time."

"You know that's not possible, don't you?" Booker just grinned at him. "Oh, so you know that. But that's not going to stop you from trying, right?"

"That's exactly right, my boy."

Charlie came out of the building without a purse, but she was no longer crying. As he drove to the pizza place, talking about anything that popped into his head, he wondered briefly if he could get into trouble by taking Robbie home.

Having Charlie call North and putting it on speaker phone, he could hear Amy in the background. The two of them were giggling about something funny, he thought.

"I've just taken one of the residents out of the Maple Street Sunshine home." North asked him why he'd do a stupid thing like that. "I'm going to adopt him."

"Adopt him? Booker, you do realize you can't adopt someone as old or older than our parents, don't you? Take the man back and—" Robbie told North that he was ten and could hear very well. "Oh well, that's different. All right. Let me look into things and I'll call you back."

Hanging up when North did, Booker pulled into the space right next to his dad's car. After pulling out the wheelchair and setting Robbie in it, they started toward the front door just as his dad came out.

"Well now. Aren't you a good looking fella. You visiting my son and his wife?" Robbie looked at him before looking back at his dad. "Booker, what's going on here?"

"Charlie and I are going to try and adopt Robbie. He's going to be your grandson. North is working on the paperwork now." Dad got down to Robbie's level, much the way he had, and they stared at one another. When his phone rang, he said he'd take it now.

"There isn't any paperwork I can find tonight. If anyone asks me why you have him, what do I tell them?" Booker told him what he'd run into at the center. "Good enough for me. By the way, if I were working as judge right now, you can bet your ass you'd be able to adopt him. I'll find out tomorrow if I've been approved. So, you guys have fun, and I'll come by tomorrow to meet him and to talk to you guys about what I've been able to find. Booker, you're doing a good thing with this."

"Good or not, I'm thrilled beyond words to have him being a part of my life. It was as if we clicked. Even Charlie seems to think the same thing." She came to him, wrapping her arms around his chest as Dad and Robbie went into the restaurant talking. "North, he's going to need everything. I don't know how he's gotten along so well at that place. Also, I need you to find the doctor that was seeing patients there before Charlie does. She might be a dead doctor if you don't find her first."

"I can do that." North laughed at whatever Amy said to him in the distance. "All right, Buddy. I'll see you guys tomorrow. I'll tell Amy what's going on, so don't be surprised if three women come to your door tonight bearing gifts."

"I won't. He's a little kid. But I think that has more to do with him not having anyone around to feed him well. I'm sure we can fatten him up in no time." North was still laughing as he hung up. "I guess we're going to have a son tomorrow. You really all right with that?"

"I've never been happier than I am at this moment." Charlie kissed him. "I'm going to check him over when we get home. I've been working hard on not doing it now. So you have to give me brownie points for that."

"I will."

Another kiss and they went into the pizza place. Dad and Robbie were sitting at the table together with their heads close. The wheelchair was pushed in the corner up by the door. Calling Mars, he asked him quickly if he had any knowledge of long term wheelchairs that he could get, and he said he'd look into it. Tomorrow. Tomorrow was going to be a big day for their newest Wilkerson.

Chapter 5

Robbie had been at their house for the past eight days. Booker didn't remember himself being so curious about everything. Booker was completely in awe of how many questions a kid could ask about just about anything and everything. Yesterday and today had been a marathon of questions. Robbie could have easily held the gold metal if it were an Olympic event. They'd been cleaning out storage lockers. All the uncles and his dad had one. His dad's just happen to be the largest of the five.

"Booker, do you think Grandda Josiah will let me take this back to your house? I'd like to put it in my window."

Taking it from him, Booker looked at the piece of art. He wasn't up on artists of any kind, but he had a feeling this piece had cost Dad quite a bit. "I don't know, son. I don't even know what it is, do you?"

"It's pretty." That's another thing he'd discovered. Kid logic was absolutely no logic at all to an adult. "I think if the sun were to shine through it, it would make the room just about bust with colors."

"What do you have there, Robbie?" Robbie handed the glass piece to his grandda. "I think I picked this up in Turkey when I was there. There might have been…ah, here it is. Yes. Turkey. It's a piece of glass that was made when lightning struck the sand. There are these groups of men that go around chasing lightning, and then finding these things in the sand. Then they take them back to their homes and paint things on them. I'd forgotten about this piece. Did you want it?"

After Robbie rolled away, Booker looked at his dad as he stared after the little boy. After saying his name several times, he finally turned to him. After a quick tight hug, Dad sat down on one of the many boxes they'd filled up.

"He's a great kid. I'd give him just about anything he wanted if he were to ask me for it. But I won't do that. I can't, actually. I'm afraid of Charlie." They both laughed. "But seriously, what am I supposed to do with all this stuff? I do want a few of the larger pieces. Like that chair there. I want that for my room. And the books. I'd forgotten I'd collected them at airports and put them away so that your mother wouldn't find them. They weren't classics, so they didn't need to be read."

"I remember her getting upset with me when I had a few paperbacks. I like the books too. But I'm enjoying the reader I got for myself. It's very convenient." Booker ran his hand over the table that his dad had collected and turned to look at him. "We've been talking around this for days now. Or at least you have. Tell me what has you so uptight. And please don't blow me off. You're making me nervous."

"I've met someone." Booker hugged his dad tightly again. "Well, that's not what I expected. I don't actually know what I was thinking you'd do, but not hug me. She's a really nice woman. We've been just having causal dinners together. I don't love her—I don't want you to think that there will be wedding bells anytime soon—but I do like her. She wants to meet you. And your family."

"I'd love that." They both looked up when Carson, in his cruiser, pulled into the lot where they were. Waving at the man, Booker noticed he didn't look all that happy. When he was close enough to talk to him, Carson shook his head. "Carson? What's going on?"

"You just keep your mouth closed, all right,

Booker? Don't engage or say anything to the contrary to what she's saying to you. Just go along nicely and this will be cleared up in no time. North, you stick to your cousin here like glue. Say nothing." They'd gathered a crowd by then, all family, including Robbie. "Robbie, son, I want you to go over there by Mars and stay out of sight. Just bear with me, guys, and this will be taken care of in no time at all. Please?"

"Yes, all right. Robbie, please go over to where your uncle is and stay with him." He asked if he was going to be all right. Carson told him he would be, on his honor as an officer of the law. "You can't get any better than that, son. Go on now. Stay out of sight."

The second car that pulled up had a woman getting out of the driver's side. She looked, what he'd heard Aunt Holly say about someone—fit to be tied. He'd looked it up. Right now he was looking at a visual of someone infuriated, fuming, and raging all in one little woman. She came up to him and looked like she was going to slap him when Carson stood between them.

"There ain't no point in violence, Doctor Kitty Byrd. He's not doing anything to drive you to hurting him." She said something about kidnapping while North wrote in his notebook. When he was poked, he read what his cousin had written down. The doctor from the center. "Booker, the doctor said you kidnapped her patients from the center today, and that she wants you to take them back. She's pressing charges against you for taking them out of there."

It hit him then, a little slower than it had North, that the woman thought her patients had been taken today, when Robbie had been with him for over a week, and the only other two people in the center had been moved to the condos the next day. She'd not known. But how was that—? Booker looked at Carson when dawning hit.

"She said you must have come into the place in the middle of the night and took the four people out of there. I'm taking you in so we can get this straightened out." North asked if he was going to read him his rights. "I am. Will you bear witness to him—?"

"You actually think this is some sort of game, Mr. Wilkerson? Oh, I know who you are. Some of the stories I've heard about you and your family are legendary. What sort of sick game were you thinking? Those people are old and infirm. What did you plan to do to them? It's not likely that you need their money." Since he'd been warned not to say anything, Booker didn't. But he listened while his rights were being read to him. "Cat got your tongue, young man? Is that what it is? I don't care how much money you have.

I'm going to own your ass as soon as I can get this before a court of law. Where are they? Where are the people that have been in my care for the last sixteen years? Tell me now."

He didn't, of course. But other things were coming to Booker as he stood there. She didn't know there had only been three in the building, she thought that Robbie was an old man, and she'd not been to the center for the last week at least. Christ, no wonder he'd been told to keep his mouth closed. She was going to be in so much trouble.

Riding to the station in the back of the cruiser, Carson had pointed at the camera on the rearview mirror only once for him to know to continue with the silence. Thoughts poured through his head at such a high rate of speed he wasn't sure which one deserved his most undivided attention. The one he kept coming back to was that she'd not known where they were for over a week. Booker wondered how much longer before that.

As soon as they were in the parking lot, he was helped out. The woman was there already, hurling names at him all the while he kept his eyes trained on his feet and followed Carson inside. As soon as he was taken back to a cell, Carson told him that North was calling Charlie, and she wasn't going to be able to come in and see him tonight.

"You need anything, Booker?" He shook his head. "Good man. All right. I'm to tell you there will be a judge in town in the morning. Also, at that time all the charges against you will be read. You understand me so far?" Nodding this time. "I have to tell you this. I've never been so happy to arrest someone as I am you. This'll be just fine. Just fine."

When Carson walked away, whistling of all things, Booker sat down on the cot. He wasn't upset, not really, but he didn't really see the humor in any of this right now. When North came back to see him, all he talked about was how badly Charlie was taking this, and they thought it better for everyone that she stayed home. Booker could just see his little wife taking on the system to get him out.

"The judge will hear the case tomorrow. I have all the paperwork you're going to need, and the phone log of the times you called. Thank you for giving me that. Also, I'll bring a suit for you to wear in the morning. And your son is just fine too. He told me to tell you he's rooting for you." Booker was afraid to ask about anything else that was going on, so thanked his cousin. "Just keep your cool. I know of all of us, you'd be the calmest during what goes on tomorrow. The shit will hit the fan."

"Thanks." He was handed a large bag and could smell the greasy fries. His belly rumbled when he realized he'd not eaten since lunch. "Take care of Charlie for me, North. All right? She and Ro—my son are the world to me, and I want them to be all right too."

The smile on North's face had him grinning back. When he left him there with two large burgers and fries with a large drink, he made himself a table on his lap and bit into the first sandwich. While he didn't normally eat this late, he was glad for the food. After cleaning up his mess, Booker laid down on the cot, wondering how anyone bigger than him could stand to lie on it, and thought about his predicament. Being arrested bothered him, but he had a feeling that as Carson and North had said to him, things were going to be just fine.

Waking up, it took Booker a few minutes to remember where he was. Not that he'd not been in a cell before—more than likely this very one. But unlike the other time, he wasn't hiding from his mother so he could heal, but he was here with charges pressed against him. He saw Shawn coming toward him with a garment bag.

"I'm back in town for one day and I have to bring you a suit so you can appear in court? Did you even have a good time that led you to be in here?" The note he was handed told him not to mention anything about Robbie or the case. Nodding, he took the suit from his cousin. "There are several things going on that we need to talk about. I know I was sent to Florida to help with the distribution of food and water after the hurricane hit. But I think there is so much more we can be doing there."

It was a safe subject. Nothing to do with anything that was going on right now. Shawn hadn't had anything going on when the need arose, and he'd volunteered to go there to help out, taking much needed supplies and food with him on a large plane.

Aunt Holly had a warehouse full of things to use in emergencies like the one in Florida. He and the other cousins had known about it, but hadn't been around when things needed to be taken to where it was needed. Mars usually went with his mom, Aunt Holly, but since she'd been murdered and Amy was going to have a baby, he stayed here. Which, as it turned out, was a good thing, as he was able to have more supplies taken when they realized that there was a need for dry towels, wipes, as well as quick convenient meals.

After he was dressed and Shawn left him for the courthouse, Booker was taken to the courthouse in a cruiser. There were a great many people waiting outside the place, and he was almost too afraid to get out of the car. Who knew what brought them there and what they'd do before he had his trial? But as soon as he was standing outside the courthouse, North joined him and he could hear the people cheering for him to win.

Going inside, he was relieved when the cuffs were taken off him. As soon as he sat down, he was asked to stand again as the judge came into the room. It was the one that had been watching their area for the last several weeks. He wondered what had brought her here, as she hadn't been scheduled to be here until the end of the month. Sitting down again, the commotion at the back of the courtroom had everyone turning. The man standing there looked official with his uniform and aides with him.

~*~

Judge Advocate General, or JAG for short, Herman Bitter thought of all the things he could do right now, and didn't regret a single moment in doing this. He was here with two assignments. One of them was to take over the courtroom having this trial today. The other was giving him such pleasure he nearly was giddy with the assignment.

"I'll be taking over." The judge sitting at the high table just huffed at him. Pulling out his credentials, he flashed them at her and asked her, what he thought was a polite demand, to remove herself from the room. When she hesitated for just a second or two too long, he had his men remove her. Another thing he was happy for, to witness this woman's firing. "If you'd allow me one moment here, we'll get started."

"What the hell is going on?" Doctor Byrd stood up and was told to sit down by the staff he'd brought with him. "This is an outrage. This is a court of law, not some place for you to come here and make a mockery of things."

"Young lady, I've been an attorney since long before you were ever a thought in your father's head. You will sit down and shut up before I have to have you put in irons." He turned to the bailiff that was standing next to his chair. "They do that still to civilians, don't they?"

"I don't believe so. But you could have her have an officer sit next to her to keep her in line, Your Honor." Nodding, he only had to point at one of the men and she was not just seated in her seat again, but she was threatened with having tape put over her mouth. "Sir. If you don't mind me asking you this, are you here for the duration of the day?"

"Yes." That was all he said, and the man seemed to understand completely — if his smile was any indication. "All right now. I'm ready. Doctor Byrd, you may speak by telling me only the facts of the situation that has me having to come here."

"I'm not sure why you are here at all, but I'll tell you what I encountered when I went into work yesterday morning. My patients were all gone. It took me nearly an hour of searching for answers before I found out that Mr. Booker Wilkerson had had them removed from my care." Herman asked if he'd removed them or taken over their cases. "They were no longer at the center where I've been working for the past sixteen years. These people have families that depend on me to care for them. They also have a list of medications that must be administered daily, and their care is my number one priority."

"I see. And this happened yesterday, you said." She said it had. "All right. One moment here. Booker, when did you remove the residents from the center? Just a general time. What time did you do this yesterday?"

Booker didn't speak until he looked at North.

"I didn't, Your Honor. I mean, they were removed, but not yesterday at any time." North leaned into his client and whispered, and Booker nodded before speaking again. "The first one was removed nine days ago at about four in the afternoon. The others were removed the next day."

"No, he lies. Of course he would, too. It's against the law for him to be kidnapping people like he did." Herman told Byrd to shut up. "You can't talk to me that way."

"I just did. Now shut up until I get back to you." He glared at her and turned to Booker again when she looked as if she was going to do as he told her. For now, anyway. "Booker, did you speak to the doctor at any time while you were removing her patients? Have any interaction with her at all?"

"No sir. I did not." Herman asked him if he'd tried to find her. "I did, sir. My wife and I searched the entire office area, as well as the rest of the center, and we were the only ones there besides the residents."

Byrd started to speak, but he only had to point at her. "All right. Now, here is where we get to the nitty gritty of things. Tell me why you were at the center in the first place. Do you have perhaps a family member there?"

"No, sir. I was there to make an inspection of the place. We'd heard earlier in the day that there were issues there, and we were assigned to go there and — " Byrd told Booker he lied again. "I don't lie. And will you please shut up. I'm talking now. One of the former residents had asked us to make sure the place was safe. With the things we were able to find out, we thought it was too unsafe for anyone to be living there. Especially since we couldn't find any staff or a doctor anywhere on the premises."

"I was out to lunch, I suppose. It could have happened." Byrd glared at Booker and then looked at him. "You're going to take his side in this simply because he has money, aren't you? Those poor residents. There is no telling what sort of hole he put them in to be deemed some sort of hero. Well, I want him prosecuted to the fullest extent of the law."

"What sort of things were you able to find out about the place in question?" Just as he had hoped, North handed him a list of the things they'd found. Not only were there pictures to go along with the lists, but there were also pictures of the desk that Doc Byrd was supposed to be at when they'd been there. "You like decorating your desk with dead plants, Doctor? This one here looks as if you've not watered it in a while. Why is that?"

"I don't like plants." He asked her why she had it. "I was given it by one of the residents. It would be rude to have not taken it."

"But it was all right for you to kill it." She didn't answer, which was no more than he expected. Herman looked back at the pictures. "Good heavens, is that a snake?"

"Yes, sir. I was told by one of the residents that there are rats there as well, but the snake usually takes care of them. If you'll also notice, the kitchen area has no stock in it. The rooms, the ones we could get into, had hot plates and bottled water there. While speaking of the rooms, there are no bathrooms in any of them, and the single bathroom in the hallway is a flight of stairs up from one of the residents."

"Thank you for this. Doctor Byrd. According to what I've been able to find out, your being there on the day you realized the residents were gone wasn't in the morning as you had indicated, but well after noon. It was, I've come to find out, the first time you'd been to the center in eighteen days. Give or take." She said that wasn't right. "Well, that's what I've found out. Now here is the real test. You said you've been working at the center for the past sixteen years. And in that time, you took care of the four people you said were taken yesterday, is that about right?"

"Yes. I know each and every one of them." He nodded. "When are you going to sentence him? I do hope soon. I need to get back to caring for those people."

"Point them out to me." She asked him what he meant. "The people you've been taking care of for the last sixteen years. They're all here. Well, three of them are. The fourth one doesn't exist. So look around this courtroom and tell me which of the people in here are the ones you cared for. Should be easy enough, don't you think? I mean, you have been seeing them daily for — let me think…sixteen years times three hundred and sixty-five days? That's nearly six thousand times. Yes, I'd think it would be a walk in the park. Point them out for me."

She turned and looked, and he did as well. Neither Booker nor North turned to look, but kept looking forward. There was a smile on their faces that had him thinking they were catching on much faster than the woman was. She pointed to the first person and he had him stand up.

"And his name?" She fudged around with that, then told him she couldn't tell him that. "You can't or you won't? Doesn't matter. The other two. Point them out so we can be done with this."

The other two, all three of them older men, were standing when she turned back to him. "Booker, if you'd be so kind as to tell me who it is you brought from the center. Then tell me where they are. If you can."

"I can, Your Honor. Mrs. Roberson is the lady in green there." She blew kisses at Booker and he smiled.

"Mrs. Yarrow is the lady in the blue hat." Herman asked about the third person. "That young man there in the wheelchair. Robbie Harley. He's been staying at my home for the past week getting much needed medical care for sores on his bottom from the broken down wheelchair he was given, as well as malnutrition. The ladies have been staying in a condo each near where I live, and my cousin, Wats, has been taking care of them, as has my wife and sister-in-law, both doctors as well."

Mrs. Roberson stood up. "I've never had it so good, Your Honor. I have me a kitchen I can use. A nice shower with plenty of hot water. No one treats me like I'm an old fool either. One of them set me up with my medication, and I take it when the alarm goes off, just like I'm supposed to. I'm sleeping better too, on account'a my meds are given to me when I'm supposed to have them. Not when someone gets around to them." Mrs. Yarrow reminded her to tell him about the groceries. "Oh, that's a blessing, I tell you. They set me and Mildred up on one of them computers, and we can order what we want to eat when we need something. Even if we want us a nice hot pizza brought out to us. I'm telling you, sir, we're living high off the hog, we are."

Byrd asked them how much it was costing them.

It was Mrs. Green that answered.

"Not a durned thing. Why, if I had known life could be so wonderful after being eighty, I might have done it sooner." Pointing her finger at Byrd, Mildred got hard in the face. "That nasty bitch there, she was never around. We helped poor Robbie out when we could, but he was heavy for us. After Mr. Montgomery died—he was another one like us—poor Robbie, he had to do for himself when it came to showers and such. Not that we were getting them any more regular than he was. That thing over there told us we should be lucky someone gave us a roof over our head after having nothing. I was a WAC in the army, sir. Served my country with honor and respect. Only to be shoved up in that place like I was nothing more than a placemat on a dingy table. Connie and me, we were good soldiers and did what we was told. That woman over there, she's about as worthless as a plug nickel if you ask me."

"And that is precisely why I was asked to come here today, ladies. Because of your service to your country. Also because of a woman who, when I was ready to not just leave the service but to end everything, knocked me around a bit, got me shook out, and set me up on my feet again." North asked him if it was Holly Wilkerson. "None other. She was, for lack of a better term, the best therapist I've ever encountered. Then and since. I was sorry to hear of her passing, and to be able to do this for her— Well, it makes me feel like I'm returning the favor that she asked of me all those years ago. To pay attention to those that served. They'd need me someday. And here I am."

Herman needed a few moments. It seemed the rest of the courtroom did as well. When he turned to the doctor, he smiled. It was the smile that had men under him shaking in their boots. Even the men with him today took a step back when he looked in their direction.

"It is my great pleasure, Ms. Katherine Byrd, to tell you that the State of Ohio and the federal government are looking into revoking your license as a doctor. Until such time as they come to a determination of what you are going to be subject to—" He slammed his fist down on the dais when she interrupted him. "Damn it, listen with your mouth shut. You will be spending the time in a federal prison, as you have been found lying to a federal officer, taking money from the veteran's office under false pretenses, and causing undue harm to men in the military, retired or otherwise. You will be taken away now."

The courtroom erupted in cheers and he joined them. As Byrd was taken out of the room kicking and screaming about her rights, Herman turned to the two men that had brought him here. First, however, he needed to thank someone else.

"Charlie Wilkerson, are you here?" She stood up. "I wanted to thank you from the bottom of my heart for contacting my office about this last night. It was and will be my greatest pleasure to have been a part of this so that I could be here to see the brothers and sons, because that is what she thought of all you young men, get some happiness. And to tell you that your mom/aunt/sister was the greatest person that ever took the oath of being a nurse."

"You're welcome. I found your name and picture in one of the many photo albums Holly put together. I didn't know why I thought you could help, but I figured if you couldn't, you'd know someone that could." He winked at her before she spoke again. "You're here to do the right thing for us too, right?"

"I am indeed." He stood up then, going from the dais to the floor. His men standing around him, Herman looked at North. "North Clayton Wilkerson. It is my greatest pleasure to award you the position of Federal Judge for the State of Ohio. In your new capacity, you will be able to hear hearings all over the United States and any governing agencies that need you. This position is bestowed upon you by Lorinda

Charlotte Wessex, deceased. She filed the application for you a few hours before she was killed. I myself cannot think of a better honor than to be able to do what she wasn't here to do. Congratulations, young man."

"What if I don't want it?" Herman only glanced at the men around him as they drew their weapons and aimed at North. "Christ, I was only kidding. Yes, I'll take it. Thank you very much."

Herman stayed in town overnight. Being welcomed into Booker and Charlie's home was a rare treat for him. The food was wonderful, as was the company. He also got to know young Robbie, and was going to put the adoption through for the young couple as soon as he got back to the base. When Charlie sat down across from him, he smiled at her. This was one smart woman.

"How long do you have to live?" He looked around, then back at her. "I've not been a doctor for all that long, but I can smell the chemicals on you. You have cancer."

"I do. Brain cancer, as a matter of fact. This was my last official duty as a service man. Then I go out to pasture to live out what is left of my life." She told him he was staying there. "No, I have a place for me on base that —"

"I didn't ask you, Herman. I said you were going to stay here. With three doctors in the family, we can make the rest of your life a good one. Robbie already thinks of you as a grandfather. The uncles all like you. And you saved my husband. I've already had a set of rooms set up for you on the second floor. There is an elevator we unearthed when the remodels were going in, so you won't have to take the stairs. Robbie thinks it's a hoot. You'll stay here with us and tell us some stories of Holly. I'm sure you know a few."

"I do."

He never let tears fall where someone could see them, but he did so now. When she walked away, telling Booker he was staying, he felt his heart take a hit hard enough to have him putting his hand over it. He'd not felt it beat that strong in a good long time.

Mingling with the family, he wasn't the least bit surprised to hear Booker tell the family he was going to be a part of their household. Laughing to himself, he thought Charlie could have done a better job of running the country then most presidents had. She was just the person he thought he needed to shake up his life from now on too.

Chapter 6

Pete loved it at this place. *Yfed yn Dywyll*. Welsh for Drink Darkly. Whomever named the place had done so with the décor in mind. It was dark, and there was only strong drink to be had. And that was what was going on with the five or so patrons when someone, a stranger, walked through the big double doors. Pete knew immediately that something had happened.

Careful to keep an eye on him through the dirty mirror over the bar, Pete knew he was an American. Not only that, but from the way he was dressed, she'd bet he was a man who had money to burn and didn't give a flying fuck who knew it. When he approached Sammy, the manager and bartender, she watched both men as the newcomer struggled with his question.

"Don't hurt yourself. He speaks English too." Nodding his thanks to her, Pete paid for her drink. Her heart was pounding hard now, and she wanted to get out of there. The man looked too much like someone she knew from her past. Then she realized what he'd said. "Can you please repeat that?"

"I'm looking for a man by the name of Pete Tolliver. Pete could be short for something else, but his grandfather has been hurt." She told him she was Pete. "I thought you were. He's doing much better. I'd say you're difficult to find, but I believe that's the point. He's been asking for you."

"Doubtful. If you came here looking for Pete then he didn't send you. He calls me by my first name. What's happened to him? Ben been knocking him around? If so, you give me an hour and I'll take care of him." The man sat at the bar with her and pulled off his hat. "You're a Wilkerson, aren't you?"

"Yes. Shawn Wilkerson." She only nodded. "Is there a reason you knew that? Or did someone tell you I was coming for you?"

"Had I known you were coming, you wouldn't have found me." He only nodded and asked for a beer. "You're the son of…let me think of her name. The one I have in my head isn't nice."

"I'm sure I've called her worse. If it's any help to you, they're all dead. My mother included. Penelope was her name. She was killed by a bunch of prison guards while trying to escape." Shawn drank down his beer and asked for another. When it was set before him, he asked her if she wanted another. Nodding, he ordered her one as well. "I'm set to be here for a week. I had other business in this area, so I told my family I'd come to look for you. How did the bitches hurt you?"

"Just like that, you believe me." He nodded and another beer was set before her too. "What's happened? At home, I mean."

"Stanley is in the hospital, but recovering well. He's a good sort, isn't he? Yes, it was Ben. He was pissed off because your grandda had the nerve to cash his check to pay his bills with it. Bastard. How is he related to you?" She told him. "I didn't know he had any other children alive."

"Ben's dad died right after Ben was born. I'm not sure how, but I'm sure it was tragic. My mom was born as a late in life kind of kid. There are nearly nineteen years difference in their ages." Shawn didn't say anything when a full Welsh breakfast was put in front of her. Asking for a second place setting, the two of them went to one of the many empty tables and sat down. "Have some. Let me see, my mom, Olivia, passed away when I was ten. Kidney failure. Thanks to Benton, my biological sperm donor. I think he spent ten or so months in prison for beating up Ma.

However, she died before Benton was freed. Then your family stepped in and not only was he their hit man, I do believe he knocked some of you kids around. I'm sorry if he did. But I wasn't there, nor would I have been old enough to do anything about it."

"I haven't seen Benton yet, he was in jail when I left. However, I've no doubt he was one part of the hit men our mothers utilized. Is that why you're here?" She told him she was working here, and hiding out. Pete noticed that both of them avoided the cockles. Cocos in Welsh, they were like mussels found on beaches all over the world. "I'm not telling you that you need to go home to see your grandda. Ben is going to be an issue, I'm sure. It's up to you. However, as I said, I'm here for another week, so maybe we can hang out. You can show me the sights."

"I'm afraid you're out of luck in this town for sights. Unless you're into castles and lots of green grass and sheep. Which, thankfully, a lot of people are" He laughed, and she decided he had a good laugh. "Also, I have to work tomorrow. If I do go back, and that's a big if, I'd need to go there and return here as soon as possible. I'm not much for living around a great many people, and I know your family is quite large. Also, you should understand something right now — I'm not easy. I'm not going to show you the sights by letting you into my bed."

Shawn looked at her, shocked for all of three seconds before he threw back his head and laughed. Pete didn't know why, but she had a feeling he didn't do that often, let mirth take him so hard. Smiling at him, not really understanding what he might have found so funny, he kissed her on the cheek and stood up.

"You're leaving?" Shawn said he had to check into his hotel and tell his family he'd found her. "Don't do that. Don't tell them anything just yet. I don't want to be pressured into going home. As much as I'd like to believe your family is nothing like your mother was, I'd just as soon not have to deal with them right now."

"I can understand that. However, believe me or not, we're nothing like them. In fact, I'd say we're more like my Aunt Holly. Did you know her?" She stood up so quickly the table jolted. "What is it?"

"You said *did* I know her. She's dead? Holly is dead?" Helping her to her seat, he sat too. Holding her hand, he told her the wives had had her killed a few months ago. She let the tears flow as he told her how she'd come to be gone. "She was...well, she was the best thing that could have ever happened to me. I'm staying in one of her homes, as a matter of fact." Pete looked at him. "That's why you're here. To check up on her home and tell me I have to get out."

"No. I am here to check on the house, yes, but not to toss anyone out. As Mars wasn't able to find out much about the place, he asked me if I'd come here to have a look around. To see what the house looked like, as well as the person running the place. I'm to understand it's a bed and breakfast, correct?" She said it was. "You send all the money via an account, then you're paid monthly. He couldn't understand why as well as it was doing, you weren't getting more money than what you were paid."

"I'm paying Holly back for a loan. And I do live there rent free. It's why I was able to send money to my grandda every month. I don't have much in the way of expenses. She's really gone?" He nodded. "Right after my ma died, Holly came to see me. I think she was on duty. The doctor had only just pronounced Ma's death, so I was pretty raw. When she sat down next to me, taking my hand into hers just as you just did, I launched myself at her, holding on to her while my heart broke."

"That sounds like her." Pete nodded, thinking about that day. "Go on, tell me how she was a part of your life. I'd love to hear it."

"My da was already out of the picture, so it had only been my ma and I. I was only a child, you see, but

Holly talked to me like I was her equal. She not only offered me a job when I was old enough, but lent me the money to not just pay for my ma's funeral, but to go to college as well. She made sure I didn't have to work while I was seeking higher education. Nor did she ever once try and take advantage of my owing her so much money. When I finished with school, I came here and began working off the money I owed her while running the B&B. I'm so sorry she's gone. You've no idea how many times over the years I called her just to hear her voice and to talk to someone. She was the only friend I think I've ever had." Shawn told her how sorry he was for her loss too. "Mars. I know him. And…let me think which one. Booker. I wasn't Pete them, but Petunia Jackson. I was adopted by my grandda when my ma died, so I'd not have to be put in the system."

"We didn't know it was a woman we were looking for. And you were right, your grandda didn't send me. I don't think he even mentioned you until we asked if there was anyone to notify. He said your name was Pete then, but no last name. Stanley said he'd contact you when he was home again." Pete told Shawn that she went by Pete so she was harder to find. "It worked. If not for an entry made on some of the notes Aunt Holly kept, we wouldn't have known you were even here in Wales."

"Holly told me I'd be safe here. And I am. However, I was never sure who I was safe from, as Ben never bothered with me. Not even after he found out I had a good job while finishing up high school." He asked her if he'd known about her. "I think so. However, now that you mention it, I have no idea. I'd see him around, of course. Know he was my cousin, I suppose. But as far as him acknowledging me, I'm not sure. That's a good point. Perhaps Holly kept me safer by just keeping me out of his line of sight."

"More than likely. Are you all right now?" She nodded, then shook her head. "I can understand that too. I've known for a while that Aunt Holly is gone, and I still have trouble coming to terms with it. She was one of the best there was."

"She was. Too a great many people, I'm thinking."

When Shawn tried to pay the bill, Sammy asked her, in Welsh, if he understood that she owned the bar. Shaking her head, she told Sammy she'd talk to him later and she left. Pete was just too raw to try and explain to anyone that she had her own money now, and she was beholden only to Holly, who had died.

Shawn followed her out of the bar. "He said something along the lines of owning. Or it could have been owing. You own the bar."

"Yes. I own the bar, as well as a coffee shop down the road. I didn't take any of the money from the B&B. I promise you that. Nor did I use any of the money then put it back. I've been—" He laughed again. "I'm a bit touchy on things, if you didn't notice it. Money and owing someone is hard on me."

"I guess I can understand that. However, it never occurred to me that you were doing that. Nor that I would ever think you would." She nodded and looked away. "How about we start over? I'm Shawn Wilkerson, nephew to Holly Wilkerson. I'm here looking for you to give you some information that your grandda—whom I like, by the way—has been hurt."

"Thank you." They shook hands and she told him she needed to get back to the B&B. Shawn followed. "Really, I can get there from here. I've been doing it for some time now."

"It just so happens I'm staying there too. In another room." She shook her head. "How about later, you and I have a nice dinner and talk about my aunt. Or anything, for that matter. I'd like to get to know you."

"I don't know. I'm very caustic." He laughed, and she smiled at him. "All right. But I cook for the patrons at the B&B. It's easier than trying to make a breakfast with all the trimmings. I usually have it for lunch and that's it. But since we shared, I'll be able to eat at dinner time."

Whatever was going on, she wasn't sure about it. However, she was going to call Mars and let him know what was going on. While she knew the other man, she wasn't sure how much he knew about her. But Booker she did know, and would also call him.

~*~

Booker was still working on a couple of projects at home when his cell rang. He knew the ringtone. It was Shawn. Since he'd heard from Shawn when he'd arrived three days ago that he'd made it, he knew whatever was going on now was something funny. Thinking of something to bust his chops about, he answered the phone with a nasty quip about his sexuality.

Charlie had gone to bed about an hour ago. Booker took into account that Shawn might not have realized the time difference. Or perhaps he did. When he realized that Shawn hadn't said anything back, he sat up straighter in his seat.

"Shawn?" He heard voices. They weren't speaking English, so he was at a loss as to what might be going on. Waiting for whoever called him using Shawn's phone, he concentrated on breathing in and out instead of what might be going on with the phone call.

"Booker Wilkerson?" He said it was him. "My name is Pete. I'm using your cousin's phone to—"

"Is he all right? Do I need to come there—?"

"Just let me tell you, damn it. You've no idea how freaked the fuck out I am right now." He could hear her speaking to someone else. While he didn't know what was being said, he figured that since Shawn had gone to Wales, they were speaking Welsh. "I'm going to be calm here. I'm having difficulty translating what I'm being told in one language, figuring it out in English to tell you, then reversing the process so I can tell the people here. Just fucking bear with me. I'm stressed the fuck out."

"All right. Can you tell me if he's dead?" She said he wasn't, but it had been touch and go for a bit. Then she said something in Welsh again. "Take your time, Pete. Just breathe. That's what I'm trying to do right now."

"He wanted to go on a run. Early morning here. There are a lot of lorries out that early, making deliveries and such." He nodded, then told her to go on. "Hang on."

His heart was hurting, but he knew if he were to scream at the woman to get her to get on with the story, he might well not learn a damned thing. Reaching for his house phone, he called Charlie's cell phone. Telling her to hurry down here, he could hear her racing down the stairs. Booker put his cell on speaker phone after telling her the little he knew. He also cautioned her to not hurry the woman along.

"The doctor here wants to know if he has any allergies to medications." He said he didn't. He was, however, allergic to caffeine. "Bear with me. I'm so upset here, and I've not spoken English for some time."

Booker looked at Charlie when she cleared her throat. "I can speak to you in Welsh if you'd like. If that would help. It's been a while for me too, so let's start out slowly."

The two of them spoke in Welsh, another thing about his lovely wife he'd not known until now. Smiling at her, he asked for Charlie's cell and called Uncle Hank.

"Booker? What's happened? Where are you?" He told him all he knew so far. "She didn't tell you what happened? Who does that? Tell her I want—?"

"She'll hang up. I don't know that she will, Uncle Hank, but she's pretty upset. Charlie is helping her now. I'm not sure what's going on, but I thought you'd like to come here. I'm making the calls now." He said he was on his way. "All right. Do you think we should call the others in?"

"Not yet. They'll just want answers we don't have. Call them when we have more. Oh, I wish I had gone with him as he wanted. I'm on my way, son." Booker put the phone down when his uncle just hung up.

Charlie turned to him. "She's speaking with the staff about his things. Shawn was out running this morning and a truck hit him. They don't think it was on purpose, as the roads are very narrow in places, and Shawn might not have been off the road far enough when another truck was passing the one that hit him." He asked if she knew how he was hurt. "He hit his head. That's all they told her when they called her. Everyone apparently knew he was staying at the B&B she is running for Mars. Oh, she knows Mars too. You know her as well, apparently. She's Petunia Jackson."

It took him a few moments to put a face to the name. When he remembered her, he could only think of her as a child. He also knew that at some time in her life, she had moved away. More than likely when she'd been that same young woman he remembered. Calling Mars, because he'd been asked to, he told him the information as well as the little bit more he knew about Shawn. He and Abby were on their way over too.

"He's in surgery. His leg was broken in four places and they're setting it. Since she doesn't know what they're doing in there, she can't tell me what sort of setting they're doing. She's stressed to the max, Booker. I think she might be blaming herself for this." Booker asked if Pete had been with him when he was running. "Not that I've been made aware of. She's running the B&B and doesn't get out much this time of year, I guess."

"We'll all end up there sooner rather than later, I'm betting." Charlie went back to the call while he let his uncle and cousin in. Mars had apparently called in the others as well, as they were coming to the house one at a time. Going into the kitchen, he wasn't the least bit surprised to see that Herman had started coffee and was making pancakes. He'd in the kitchen for the past couple of days whenever he wanted to talk to him.

"I still have some pull, so I called to see what is going on over there. So far I'm only waiting on a call. I wasn't snooping, but I could hear the doorbell ringing and figured something—hang on, that's my contact now." Sitting at one of the chairs around the big table, Booker pulled a pancake to him and rolled it around a piece of sausage. While waiting, he also poured him some juice. "All right. A young man was hit by a truck at five their time this morning. So there is a five hour difference — they're ahead of us — so I'm thinking it happened sometime around midnight our time. Someone must have been with him to have him in the hospital very quickly if that is the case. He wasn't just left there to die. What I mean is, he wasn't left on the side of the road. That didn't come out right either."

"I understood. The woman we're talking to over there, she runs my cousin's B&B. I know nothing about her, but I'm guessing she and Shawn were friends." Herman simply shrugged. He was talking to someone on the second phone call he'd gotten. When he continued to nod, Booker got up and started pulling glasses from the cabinet. When the call was finished, Herman said he had good news. "Good. I could use it about now. I'm sure everyone will be happy for it too."

"Shawn's leg is busted up pretty badly. They've had to reinforce two bones with some steel rods. He's going to be a long time in healing. The head wound wasn't as bad as they had thought. Of course he'll have a major headache for some time to come, but he'll be all right. Two of his fingers are broken, as well as his wrist. All on the left side." He asked what was going to happen now. "They'll keep him sedated for a few days, just to let the swelling go down. The young woman, Pete, is the granddaughter of Mr. Tolliver. He adopted her when she was just a young child. Monthly she sends him nearly her entire pay to keep him afloat. Also, she's done well with investments too. She not only owns the bar, but a coffee shop as well as a bun store. I had to ask, it's just sweets."

"We all thought she was a man." Herman nodded as he put another round of batter on the griddle. "I'll call the others in to get some food. You can tell them what you know and we'll go from there."

As everyone stood around eating pancakes and sausages, they talked about going to Wales to see to Shawn. When Charlie joined them in the kitchen, having been speaking to Pete, she told them what she'd been able to find out.

"The B&B is full until the end of the week, so we can't stay there. Also, there aren't any hotels or other accommodations within four hours of the hospital. Pete suggested we wait until Friday before we travel there and the place will be all ours. This time of the year they close up for a month to have the carpets cleaned, as well as any upgrades that are needed." Mars said he'd read that in some of the notes on the place. "She's much calmer now. The doctor told her that Shawn would need to rest for the next few days, so they've put him into a medically induced coma. I agree with her on the fact that we can't do anything until he wakes. She said she'd call us whenever there was any news, and she'd be using his phone, as she has no cellphone of her own. You might be interested to know that she and Shawn have been seeing the sites. I haven't any idea what that might entail, but they have been hanging out together."

"You think she's his future wife?" Charlie smacked him on the arm. "I was only asking. I mean, it's a long way to go to find someone to love, but—you don't think she'll make him live there with her, do you? Mars, you have to fire her or something. We can't lose Shawn to another country. How will our kids get to know one another?"

"Cool your jets, dumbass. You've already got them married with children. How about we just figure out how to get there and when, and we'll work from there. As far as we know, she's a royal…well, she is a royal bitch, but that's all right too. We'll not rush into anything for now." Booker smiled at Charlie. "I haven't any idea what you might be thinking, but it's not going to bode well for you if I have to smack you around a little in front of your family. Behave."

"But it's so much more fun to not behave." She smacked him again, harder this time, and he pulled her into his arms for a much needed kiss. "We will need to make arrangements to get there. Not only will we need to have passports, but time off from work for this. I can do my work anywhere, but I know a lot of us can't."

The rest of the morning was spent talking about the trip, what they'd need to be taking, and calling bosses or whatever they had to take care of while they'd be gone. Wats told them with an injury like Shawn's sounded, it might be a month before he'd be up from the bed. That was when Mars decided he'd charter a plane, take them there, and bring Shawn home when they could. It was a plan everyone agreed would work better. Then Herman cleared his throat.

"Two things you must remember. You'll need to have cash, as credit cards might be all right, but this is a smallish town and they might have poor Internet. The second thing is, not only will you need passports, but you might also need to have some proof of Shawn being related to any of you. Hank, I would suggest that you take everything you have concerning his birth records. As well as taking a death certificate of your wife. Just to make things go smoother. Also, I just remembered this, you'll need an attorney in the States in the event you need something else. An attorney can make things move faster. Having one ready to go, with knowledge of where and why you're going, will save time as well." North was making notes and asking questions about some things he had questions about. The rest of them, even for as many attorneys that were in the family, just waited to see if they needed to do anything too. "I just realized that you have three qualified physicians in the family. Medical certification should be handy if needed. Also, this is very important, don't step on toes. I know you won't mean to, but it'll do better for young Shawn if he's not the center of a national debate on US doctors versus any in Wales."

"I agree on that one." Wats told them how he'd been in another state and had offered his help at a very busy hospital following a traffic pile up. "They were nasty, so much so that they called security on me. I learned a very valuable lesson in that."

By the time everyone was headed back to their homes, they'd made some real headway in getting things ready to go. Hank was going to leave this afternoon to be with his son, while the rest of them waited until they could have accommodations. As it was now, there was very little they could do but watch Shawn sleep, and that would drive them all nuts, Booker thought.

As he was headed up to bed to take a shower, Booker realized he'd been up for too long for him not to take a nap. Just lying on the bed, hoping for at least an hour of rest, he thought of Shawn being so far away. Of all his cousins, he and Shawn were the closest to each other. He thought it had a lot to do with the order of their birth. They were only about two months apart, while the others were as much as six months.

Almost as soon as his head touched the pillow, his body began to shut down. He knew, in that moment, that this wasn't going to be a nap, but he'd sleep for at least several hours.

Chapter 7

Charlie checked her patient three times before she simply stood back and asked what had brought her in to the office today. Everything about the woman screamed anxiety. Whether it was at her or something else, she didn't know. But when she looked around and lifted up her long sleeved sweater, Charlie had a feeling she was needing more than just her help to stitch up a cut.

"He said I could come here and have it stitched up, but I was to keep my mouth shut." The whispered statement had her leaning closer to the other woman to hear her. "I'm betting he's at the door right now."

"He'd better not be." Just to see, she went to the door and opened it quickly. The man nearly tumbled into the room. "Excuse me, what are you doing?"

"I'm making sure you're not talking her into something." Charlie asked him what he thought she could talk anyone into. "I know your type. You think there is something going on that you need to be rescuing someone from. Well, you're wrong. There isn't anything going on between us other than she fell and cut her arm."

"She said she cut her arm while cutting up lettuce for your salad." He said that was the other time when she fell. "I see. Actually, I don't care how she did it. You're to go to the waiting room, like everyone else does, and stop listening at doors. A shut door means you're not welcome inside, not for you to be standing outside of it ready to pounce. Go, before I have to have you kicked out to the curb."

He didn't like it, but he did go to sit in the waiting room. As he was leaving the room, he looked hard at her patient and did that finger to his eyes things— telling her, Charlie supposed, that he'd be watching. Well, she was as well. Going to find Adilene to get a kit to sew up Shannon's arm, she also let her know to call in Carson, just to make sure everyone on this end was aware of the issue that may be going on.

Carson showed up just as she was wrapping the wound on Shannon's arm. He was dressed in his street clothing, and she had a feeling he'd done that on purpose, so as not to draw attention to himself or what he was doing.

The wound had required twenty-three stitches, and a great deal of tears. While she was working on her arm, the younger woman told her how the man she had been living with wasn't her husband as he claimed. He had decided, she told her, that her home was bigger than his, and one day when she came home from work, not only had he moved into her home, but he had changed the locks on the house as well as putting a lock box in the living room, where her phone and her car keys were to go until he allowed her to go out.

"Are there any other relatives you can call? I'm not saying you should leave your house, miss, but there has to be someplace you can go until we get him arrested. Someplace safe." Carson had also been whispering since he'd shown up. Adeline had let him in the back door so Bud, the man, didn't know he was there.

"No. I live in the houses out on Trinway Road. The places the government helps people like me buy. My boy, he's staying with his father until Christmas, but I'm fearful of him coming home to this, to be honest. I'm afraid Bud will hurt him. Or use him against me."

Charlie thought that was a good possibility.

When someone pounded on the door, Charlie laid the gauze over Shannon's arm to make it look like she was still wrapping it. Opening the door, she asked Bud what he wanted. He looked pissed off. She was glad Carson had hidden behind the door when she'd opened it.

"You know, every time I have to stop what I'm doing and see what you want is taking all that much longer. Will you just go sit down and leave me to my work? I've enough going on without you pounding on my door too." Wats came out of the room he'd been in and asked if something was going on. "This man here is coming into the room every ten minutes to hurry me along. I'm wondering if he has a date or something. I can't finish up with all this going on around me."

"Mr. Findley, why don't you have a seat and stop bothering Doctor Wilkerson? Or better yet, why don't you go out there and pay some on your bill? The last time you were in for that little problem of yours, you didn't pay some on the bill as you said you would." Wats put his arm on Bud's shoulder. Pushing him more than just being nice, the man was shoved down the hall and to the front desk. "Adeline, Mr. Findley is going to make a payment. If he doesn't, then call my attorney. His bill is piling up on us."

"He's going to be a while." Carson nodded. "Now what do we do? I mean, she can't go back home with him. He's pissed off enough now that he may well hurt her."

"Shannon, I want you to come with me. I'm going to put you in a jail cell for a bit until I can get you someplace safe. I'm thinking with one of the Wilkersons, but we'll get there. He'll not get to you there." She nodded, willing, it seemed, to get this finished. "Is the place you're staying in your name, or both of yours and Bud's?"

"Mine. Just mine." Carson nodded and smiled. "Is that going to be all right? I mean, I'd really hate to be tossed out. I really want to own a home for my son and I."

"It'll be just fine, I promise you. He didn't have permission to move into the place with you, I'm assuming?" She shook her head. "Good deal. All right. We're going to go out the way I came in. The back door. Charlie, if you could give Wats a call, see if he knows of a place Shannon can hide out, that would be great."

"There is room at my home." Carson told her that would be the first place Bud would look. "I guess he would. I'll call him now while you get out of here. I'm going to go up front to tell Adilene that I have to take a couple of X-rays as your arm is a bit swollen, Shannon, so you wait right here until I'm gone. I'll make sure Bud isn't in any way able to see down the hall."

Charlie was still walking toward the front desk when she heard the door behind her open, then close. The second, outer door did the same, and she was glad they were out of the building. Telling Wats she wanted to take a couple of pictures of Shannon's arm, he agreed with her, telling her there was no point in having to do this a second time if something else happened.

"Is she going to be much longer? Christ, had I known it was going to be an all day event, I'd have just kept her at home. I'm hungry." Wats, usually not so vocal with his patients, told Bud to shut up or he'd shut him up. "You got yourself a good bedside manner there, Doc. I just wanted to know if my wife was going to be taking all day."

"She's not your wife, is she? I mean, when she signed herself in, she wrote Shannon Vickers." He said he was working on convincing her that they needed to be married. "That'll be a shame. She'll lose out on that nice house if you marry her."

"What's that? What do you mean, she'll lose the house? It's a nice one. Three bedrooms and all. What do you mean she'll lose it if she's married?" Wats explained it to him. "No kidding? They'll make her give it up on account'a me adding to the income? Well, I guess I need to quit my job then. I don't want to lose that nice house. It has a washer and dryer, so she don't have to drag my clothing to the mat no more. Also, and I love this one the best, she has all the cable too. While she's gone to work, I sure do have a good lot of fun watching cable all day. I was going to have her work a bit harder to get us one of them giant screened televisions."

Charlie wanted to smack the man upside the head, but she did take some pleasure in knowing Shannon was getting away. When he went on about how the house was so nice and warm right now, she had to leave the room. Going to her office, closing the door, she called Booker.

"I've made arrangements to have your passport ready in the morning. Herman helped with that. He's not going with us, so you know. Neither is Robbie. They're going to hang out with your grandda while we're gone, as well as watch the houses. We're set to leave the day after tomorrow. Also, and this one I get the biggest kick out of, Mars bought a plane. He said it was so much cheaper to do that than to rent on for the duration. Also, he's going to have the back fixed up so when Shawn does come home with us, he'll do it in style. How's your day going?" She told him about Bud and Shannon. "I know her. Shannon Dailey. She's a cute little thing. Or she was when I'd see her around town. I think she has a little boy about Robbie's age. Her parents were very controlling, if I remember right."

"She's been hooked up with one just like them, I think. Bud Findley is bragging how he's going to have to quit his job so she can stay in the house. Moron." Booker laughed. "What would you say to gathering up our little family and having a nice night out? Herman has been cooking most of the meals when Mae is off, or they work together. They seem to do that well enough. I think Herman needs to feel like he's paying us back or something. So, I'm betting they both could use a break. However, I know that neither Mae nor her husband will agree to go with us. And I love the look on Robbie's face when we mention going out. That kid. I have to tell you, having him around is like a breath of fresh air."

"Good idea on the dinner plans. I'll see what I can find. Also, you got something in the mail today. I'm not sure what it is, but I'm thinking it's your diploma." She squealed and he laughed. "That's another reason for us to go out and celebrate. My wife is a full fledged doctor. All right, love. I'll talk to you later. If you need me, just call."

One of the first things North had done when he was sworn in as judge was to marry the two of them in a short but sweet ceremony. Then, after Herman had signed off on the paperwork for them to adopt Robbie, they were officially a family. Now they were a houseful, and there was nothing she'd do to change a thing, other than to have a child of her own. Thinking of which, she went into her bathroom to check on the pregnancy test she'd left there an hour ago.

"Well, poop." She looked up when someone came into her office. Handing the test to Wats, he laughed. "I don't think this is funny, my dear sir. I was hoping to be able to tell Booker tonight that we're having a baby."

"This one of the tests from the box in the other office?" She nodded. "Those expired four years ago. I meant to tell you that, but with everything going on, it slipped my mind."

"Can you run a test for me now?" He nodded. "Is Bud still here? Mars is going to put Shannon up in one of the condos for now. Adeline told me."

"No, he's left. Carson came by again and took care of it. They're moving him out of her house now. He's not the least bit happy about the turn of events not going in his favor." Wats drew blood to run the test. "Also, you should be aware that he's not blaming you. He said she'd been trying to run off for days now, and I quote, when he's such a good catch. Sometimes I think there are no sane people in the world."

"I agree with you." He said he'd run this now. "Thanks. You won't tell him, I know that, but I'm sort of on the fence about having a baby now. I want one, but the timing isn't the best. Now with Shawn being — What the hell was that for? You hit me in the head."

"I did. What do you think Shawn would say if he were to find out you were upset about having another Wilkerson because he was hurt? He'd hit you harder. Then he'd be upset with himself, but he would hit you." She smiled at him. "I'll know here in a few minutes. But get that thought of timing out of your head."

She said she would. "What's the result? Please please tell me." He smiled. "I'm going to have a baby?"

"Well, your hCG levels are up." She knew what that meant. It was the one question she missed on her doctor's exam. Human Chorionic Gonadotropin. She could be pregnant. "Don't tell him yet. I'll do another test in…well, before we leave for Wales. If they're up more, then we'll know for sure."

Kissing him on the cheek, she danced around the office. Having a child of Booker's couldn't have been more wonderful. Going home, taking a shower, she ran her hands over her still flat belly. A baby could be growing there, and she was suddenly too excited to not tell Booker. But she wouldn't. They still had plenty of time to celebrate, and she was going to make it a slam dunk celebration when she told him.

~*~

Pete was exhausted. She also thought if she had to eat one more plate of hospital food, she'd just give up eating altogether. When Mr. Wilkerson came in with what smelled to her like heaven, it was all she could do not to knock him to the floor and eat whatever was in the bags he'd brought in.

"I thought you'd enjoy a treat. I know I would." He started laying out the covered plates of food. "Sammy, the man at the bar you frequent, said you usually only eat at the place once a day, but when you can eat there more often, it's his famous fish and chips."

"It's the best there is. How much do I owe you, Mr. Wilkerson?" When he didn't move, his hand about halfway to her, she looked up at him. "What have I done? Whatever it is, I'm sorry. I'd do anything for the food."

"Then call me Hank." She said she couldn't do that. "Sure you can. It's a one syllable word. Try it. Hank. It's completely common name. Something that my wife, when she was around, tried to get me to change often enough. Anyway, I'd very much like for you to call me Hank. Please?"

"Mr. — Hank, you're only here for the short time it's going to take to get your son home. I know that. You don't really have to be nice to me. I like Shawn, but again, he was only here to tell me about my grandda, then he was leaving." Hank asked her how sure she was about that. "What do you mean?"

"Honey, I've seen the way you look at him. I hear you crying when you think no one is around. You're in love with him. It's as plain as the nose on your face." She said that wasn't possible, as she'd only known him a few days before he'd gotten hurt. "With my nephews, that's all it took for them to fall in love with their wives. My goodness, Mars and Abby knew each other less than any of them before Mars asked her to marry him. Now there is a good young man. I sometime think how much I missed of his life too."

He'd told her about his sister being murdered. How the wives of him and his brothers had conspired to not just have her raped, then murdered, but they had pitted them all, including their father, against her. She thought they were about the most fucked up family she'd ever encountered. But she did like Hank.

When he'd arrived two days ago, she had picked him up at the airport to take him to the hospital. The first thing he asked her was if she was all right.

Nodding, as her emotions had gotten the better of her, he hugged her tightly and cried with her. Since then he'd been staying in her room while she bunked in the apartment over the bar. She liked it there better anyway, as there were not that many people around.

The doctor came into the room with them then and told them he was grateful for the extra food for the staff too. She'd not known he'd done that, but he included her in saying they'd both decided they worked too hard and deserved a treat as well. Translating for Hank was getting easier all the time. But she did appreciate when the doctor spoke English for him.

"Shawn is mending well. The pins in his leg to keep it stable aren't causing any damage to his skin. At times we do run into a little bit of trouble with infection getting into the wounds, but that isn't a problem thus far." Hank asked about his other wounds. "We did an X-ray of his head again last night. There isn't any swelling, nor do we foresee any future trouble with that. He'll have a headache when he wakes, but nothing more that a couple of ibuprofen won't take care of."

"Will he be able to walk again? It looks frightening with all this going on with his leg." Pete was embarrassed for asking such a cruel question, but

Hank said he'd like to know that as well. The staff had long since given up on getting her out of the room when they talked about Shawn with Hank. He had insisted, and she stayed. "I mean, I don't know him all that well, but he seems to be a very active person."

"He is. Shawn has been a runner for a long time. I say that because I've noticed he goes out several times a day. He told me it was to clear his mind. I can see that." She smiled at Hank. "I'm sorry. What else do we need to know about my son?"

"I'm going to start lowering his medication to have him waking soon. He'll be in and out of consciousness, but that's to be expected. Also, you shouldn't expect him to remember what happened right away. Don't force his memories. Just let them come to him a little at a time." Hank said they'd do that and reached for her hand to hold. "Once he's awake fully, in a few more days, we'll do more tests on him and see where we stand about his walking. I know he will be able to, but I don't want to make any promises right now on how active he'll be once we remove the pins."

After the doctor left, Hank left her to call the family. There wasn't much in the way of service for cell phones in Shawn's room, so she just stared at the man she'd come to love. Not that she'd admit that to anyone but herself, but she wanted so desperately for him to wake up. Like she did whenever they were alone, she spoke to him.

"Your father is very nice. He's trying very hard not to be too worried about you, but I think he'll be all right." She took his hand into hers and was glad to feel warmth in it. "You do know I'm going to beat you senseless when you wake up. I might wait a couple of days to do it, but I did tell you, several times, to be extra careful at crossings. You shouldn't have been on that stupid bridge."

Standing up, she went to the window and looked out over the beautiful landscaping. It would be easier to talk to him this way. Even though she knew he couldn't hear her, she still wanted to tell him things she wasn't sure would make him happy with her.

"I don't just run the B&B for your cousin. Nor do I only own the bar and coffee shop. There are several pieces of property I own that I rent to farmers. I can do this because I have a job. One that I work at from wherever I'm putting my hat at any given moment." She drew in a deep breath and let it out slowly. "You see, I write. Books. Of course. That was stupid. I write books that are racy. Well, I think they're more than racy, but that's just me. Anyway, I have been writing since I was in high school. Just playing around. Then

I submitted one of my stories to one of the smaller publishing houses for fun. It wasn't two days later that I was called by the person in charge, the owner, and she asked me if I had any more stories. I never call them books. To me it sounds like I'm being pretentious. She and I hit it off really well, and I've been doing it since then. I don't want you to think badly of me—"

"Why do you think he'd think badly of you?" She turned so quickly she nearly fell over. "Be careful there, child. You don't want to be laid up too, now do you? But answer my question. Why do you think Shawn, or anyone for that matter, would think badly of you for using a talent to make money?"

"They're dirty books." Hank laughed. "I don't think it's funny. What do you think his friends or his family is going to say when they find out I'm nothing more than an author that writes books for a living?"

"I think they'll tell you they want a copy of them. Are there a great many of them?" Pete told him how many she had published at last count. "Oh my. Yes, oh my indeed. That's quite a few of them, honey. Good for you. They'll be so happy to know that. Especially the women of the family. I know for a fact that Abby reads—I believe she calls them bodice rippers. I'm assuming you don't write under Pete Tolliver."

"No. Just my first name. No last. It makes things

easier for me." He laughed and went to his phone. When he found whatever it was he was looking for, he handed it to her. "Which one of your—? She has my book."

The woman in the picture was asleep on a couch. On her lap was one of Pete's earlier books. Right there on the cover was her name in script, Petunia. Handing him back his phone, she didn't know what to say to him now.

"I'd say they're going to be— Pete, look at Shawn." She did. He was staring at her with wide eyes. Not moving, she was glad when Hank went to his son, saying his name. As soon as Shawn turned to his dad, Pete felt as if she'd run a marathon. Twice over.

There were monitors all over his body. Also a feeding tube in his nose. Since he'd been out for so long, they wanted to make sure he was getting enough nutrients. Going out into the hallway to tell the nurses, it took her several deep breaths for her to get her shit together.

Pete went in behind the nurses. The doctor had been called in as well, they told them. When she moved back out of the way, Shawn put out his hand and she took it. The connection, or whatever it was, made her feel like she'd been given a new outlook on life. A steady stream of tears blurred her vision, but she was so very happy to see him awake.

They worked with him for about twenty minutes before they left him again. The nurses did tell Shawn not to fight the rest he needed. When he closed his eyes, she started to pull her hand free and he tightened his grip. She sat that way with him while Hank went out to call his family again.

"You scared us." Opening his eyes again, he winked at her. "Go to sleep before I have to knock you out. But know this—if you ever come to visit again, you're not going to go running in the middle of the night."

"Daytime." She pointed out that it was still dark when he'd gone out. "Am I all right now?"

"I'm not a doctor, dummy." He smiled with his eyes closed again. "You're going to be just fine. Your leg is busted up pretty good, but I can't see you letting that get you down much. You're supposed to be sleeping, not having me tell you stuff you can find out from your dad."

"He'd lie to me." She figured she should have too instead of telling him she was going to knock him around. "Thought of you when the truck hit me. Thought of you being pissy."

When she was sure he was asleep, she laid her head on his hand holding hers. She'd been so stressed for the last couple of days she'd not really been sleeping all that well. Just thinking she'd close her eyes for a moment, Pete yawned once more and let her body relax enough to take her under.

Waking up when someone touched her, she had to take a couple of moments to remember where she was. Hank asked her if she felt better, and with a glance to Shawn, who was still sleeping, she told him she was all right.

"You've been asleep for nearly five hours like that. I was sure you'd be hurt when you woke up. Must be your youth that keeps you from cramping up like I think I would." She asked him if she'd really been asleep for that long. "Yes. The only reason I woke you now was because they're going to take Shawn down for a couple of more X-rays of his arm and hand. I can only think you needed it."

"I guess I did." Standing up, she was stretching when the orderly came to get Shawn. "Do you know how long this will take?"

"No, ma'am. There are a couple of people ahead of your husband, but it won't be that long." She started to explain she wasn't Shawn's wife, but after a glance at Hank and him shaking his head, she let it go. "If you've a cell phone, I could give you a call if you'd like to go out. It's a lovely night tonight. Might get some of the cobwebs out of your head for a bit."

After agreeing that would be wonderful, Hank gave the young man his cell number. Going down in the elevator, she did feel better, she realized, and was so happy to be outside in the really nice night. Taking in a deep breath, she closed her eyes and let all her stress just wash off her.

"The family will be here tomorrow. I noticed that the patrons at the B&B have left today too. Will you move back to the house?" She told him that with his family coming, they'd be packed up. "I suppose. But I hate that we're putting you out of your home. You have more right to it than we do."

"It's not my home. It's Mars's, and I guess now Abby's. But I'm all right over the bar. Sammy feeds me and makes sure I'm not bothered. There isn't a phone up there, but I'm all right with that as well. It's very quiet." She smiled at him. "I'll be by to make dinner for everyone if they want. I've become quite the Welsh cook over the years."

Pete wasn't keen on seeing the rest of the family. Not that she was going to have much choice in the matter, but she really wished they'd just allow Hank to take care of getting his son home. He was, like his son, a very nice person. She wished they'd met under entirely different circumstances. But then, without

Shawn being hurt, they might well have never met at all.

"There's our signal."

She was happy to be going back in. They'd have a little more information from someone, and that was good. As they were seated Shawn came into the room, bed and all, and she could tell he was in a great deal of pain.

"He's a bit on the stubborn side, mistress." She asked what had happened. "He thought he could lift himself up and onto the table when he's not strong enough just yet. I've asked the nurse for something for his pain."

She told Hank what the young orderly had told her. He'd been so nervous, she supposed, that he had slipped into speaking his own language. Pete glared at Shawn while the drugs from the nurse hit his system and he began to relax.

"What do I have to do? Go with you everywhere so you behave? Didn't I tell you to be careful?" He smiled, but she was on a roll. "I'm not going to stand for you making your father upset again, do you understand me?"

He looked at his dad, then back at her. "I have no idea what you just said but for a couple of words. You're upset, I get that. However, if it's about me moving myself, you should have seen the little bitty thing that was trying to lift me up to put me near the machine. And she was several months pregnant." She told him that was what she was upset about. "I'm sorry I upset you too. That's the last thing I wanted to do. But I can't allow someone smaller and very pregnant to lift me when I can move myself."

"And how did that work out for you? You hurt yourself by being all macho."

He threw back his head and laughed. She had to join him, it was just too infectious for her not to. Even Hank joined the two of them.

Chapter 8

Booker loved the house. Really, it had been three houses turned into one. But it flowed well and worked very well for guests of the B&B to not just have plenty of room, but also to find a spot to be alone. Mars joined him in the solarium.

"This didn't look like this according to the paperwork I had my attorney give me. There are pictures of the place, but it's a good deal larger than it shows in them." Booker asked Mars if his mom had done that. "I don't think so. I think Pete saw a need and ran with it. I'm sure she talked to my mom about it before doing it. But there isn't any mention of the improvements on any of the paperwork I have. I love this."

Booker handed him the photos when he asked for them. "The kitchen in this picture is way smaller. I don't think they could have gotten any tables in here but the one in the corner there. It looks like instead of just opening the place up by putting in a garden between these two houses, the entire lower half of the two buildings has been made a dinning and kitchen area." He and Mars walked outside to face the front of the buildings. "Christ, Mars, she not only tripled the size of this place, but she also put in more than triple the amount of rooms. And according to the book I saw in the office, they use every one of them all the time too."

"That's not all. When she closes the place down for the month, like she is now, she has all the carpets cleaned, painting done where it's necessary, as well as has the linens and other things in the rooms redone every two years. That way if someone comes back here to vacation, they have a fresh look." They walked to the building on the other side of the breakfast place. "This room, according to what I've been able to find out, is for the resale of the items she takes out. If a guest comes in and falls in love with the décor, it's not only sold to them, but there is such a mark up on it that Pete is able to make the room look as if nothing had been taken out. This is a goldmine, if you ask me. Whatever isn't sold off to anyone that stays, she puts it in this shop at a great markdown for the townspeople to purchase. It's a win-win for everyone. And you know what else,

I can't find anywhere in the books that says she takes any of the money from any of these extra ventures. The detailed sales I get from her monthly state every penny she has earned."

"She's been working here for how long?" He told him eight years. "Mars, if you don't up her wages or give her a hefty bonus and part of this venture, I'm going to kick your ass. You're making a mint off this place, simply because she's thinking outside the box."

"Can I help you?" Booker knew who she was immediately. He'd not had a face to put to the name he'd been given, but seeing her now, with those big beautiful green eyes, he knew they was standing in front of Pete Toliver. "I'm sorry if you're thinking of staying. The inn is closed up for the next month." She eyed the two of them hard. "You're the Wilkersons. I know Booker a little, but you, I'm not positive about."

"Mars, Holly's son. And I'm Booker, my dad is Josiah." She shook both their hands. But it was him that praised her for doing such a lovely job on the place. "The rooms are lovely without being overdone. I might even end up with a couple of the rooms things before my wife is—"

"My mom. She had a picture of you. It was obviously a long time ago, but you and her are standing in front of a building. This one, if I remember correctly. You've grown up since then." She told him she'd been sixteen when the picture had been taken. She had a copy of it as well. Then she told him she was sorry for the death of his mom. "She would have loved to have been here with us. If for no other reason that to see how much you've improved this place. It's really beautiful."

"Thank you. I used to send her ideas about how to expand, but she'd send them back with a blank check to get it done. She also is responsible for a great many of the town's families being able to afford to send their kids off to school. I only hired locals to do the work. They did better than I expected, so this is all on them." Pete looked uncomfortable with the compliments. "This close down we're going to renovate the building behind the place for a venue place. I haven't spoken of it to anyone, as I've not heard anything from you about it. I'm assuming you would be the one to talk to about it now."

"Yes. No. I mean, we'll have the same way of working that you had with my mom, if you'd not mind." She told him she'd keep a running total so he'd not think it was out of boundaries. "No. I don't need that. In fact, I don't think I'm paying you nearly enough for what you're doing for us. Christ, Pete, this place is amazing. And for you to have so many visitors without much in the way of attractions around, but for nature, shows me you also have an amazing online presence as well."

Booker had never seen Mars so impressed with someone before. He was gushing all over Pete, and she was clearly uncomfortable with it. When she looked at him with pleading in her eyes, he laughed a little before talking to Mars.

"Mars, you're scaring her to death. Back off or you'll be running this place all by yourself." Mars snapped his mouth shut with an auditable click. "I was wondering something, Pete. You said you use locals for the work. Do they help you around the place as well?"

"The store mostly. And once a room is empty again, they will come in and clean up for us. Sheets are only changed every three days. That way I can save the place on water and electricity. It's all done here, as is most of the other things that come with a stay." She told him how they weren't able to get Internet in the building.

"Brandon is here with us. Perhaps you can talk to him what it is you need, and he can work on getting you set up while he's here. That is, if Mars doesn't mind."

"No. That's a wonderful idea." They were

entering the building when Charlie joined them. She had a book in her hand and said she was going to go out and enjoy the evening. Something bothered Pete, but Mars spoke up before he could figure out what was going on. "I think that while I'm here, we really do need to sit down and have a conversation about this place. You're not making nearly enough money for all you do. And I love the fact too that you're using locals when you find a need. All things my mom would have wanted too."

"She was such a wonderful person. I know you know that, but she made it so I could go to college as well as grow up around here. This place is my home now."

Mars and Pete went into her office. Booker looked around the place again and saw a tin on the counter, and wondered if he had found cookies. He was starving right now.

The tiny was indeed full of cookies, but they weren't anything he had ever tasted before. Biting into one of the smallest ones, which wasn't really saying much as they all looked big to him, he moaned at the taste.

"Those are Welsh cakes. With currants. Some of them had blueberries, but they're all gone now. Would you like a cup of tea?" He nodded at the woman coming into the kitchen with him. "I'm Mrs. Baker. I work for Miss Pete when she has a houseful. My goodness, now that I think on that, 'tis about weekly."

"These are amazing." She laughed and handed him a plate to put the three he had in his hand on. "If Mars finds out about these no one in the house will get anymore of them."

"I'm sure we can fix him up with a few of his own." While the water sat on the stove, she pulled down another tin. "These are the strawberry ones. I have to put them away after the miss cooks them or she'd eat them all at once. Then she'd be sick as can be after."

He took one of those and decided he'd have to fight Pete for them. Or he'd have her bake some for him. As he enjoyed his tea with Mrs. Baker, she told him about the little town and how they were all benefiting from Ms. Wilkerson's generosity.

"Mars, that's her son, is talking to Pete now about a few more upgrades to the place." She said they'd be able to fill them. "I'm sure you would. I don't mean to be indelicate, but you are aware that Holly Wilkerson passed away, aren't you?"

"Didn't know until the other day. It hurt the miss something terrible when young Shawn told her. We don't get much in the way of news here without the Internet coming in. I suppose she could go to the bar, they have the Internet there, but it's not here. Something about old wiring and the houses being so old too. I just love this part of the town." He told her he did as well. "The charm of this place is wonderful too. I've, my husband and I, have been to London to stay in a few of the dine and sleep places there, but they're over done. Too much—well, my husband, he called it fluff. Probably would be for all men, but to me, it was as well. Which room do you and your missus have?"

"The room down at the end of the first floor hall." She told him it was called Jacobson's room. "Why is it called that?"

"Oh my, that's a good story. Every year at the schools hereabout, everyone enters a contest to create a room. The theme and things, as well as colors to be used. Oh goodness, it is a great deal of fun for all of us. Jacobson Tayler, he thought the room would be wonderful if it were decorated in earth tones with a bit of the area inside for fun. The colors he picked out were perfect, and him collecting all the shells around the room helped his cause too. I would imagine that next contest we'll have all sorts of collections to help decorate with." He asked when that started again. "The rooms here were done up for this year. She's a season ahead, you see."

"But there is more to just winning the name and décor of the place as a prize, isn't there?" Ms. Baker laughed and said he was right. "Tell me what it is, please?"

"Well, they get to spend one night with their family in the room they decorated. Even if the family is a large one, which most are around here, she puts them up. Then she takes the families out to dinner in celebration. You'd not believe the pictures we have for that."

An hour later Booker was looking at the picture albums, much like the ones that Aunt Holly would put together. There were signatures on some of them. Little sticky notes on other. But in everyone of them was the family and Pete smiling and having a wonderful time. When Charlie came back in the house she joined him looking at the photos. Not just of the families either, but there was an entire album filled with the renovations of every part of the place they were staying.

Mars and the other joined them too. Pete, with Ms. Baker, fixed them their dinner, and the books weren't put away but stashed in a place they could continue looking at them after their meal. Not only was the food good, but Pete gave him his own tin of strawberry Welsh cakes to not have to share.

There was plenty of tea and local honey to go

with dinner. Conversation flooded, much like it did at home. Pete joined them after the meal. He did wonder if she'd eaten anything, and laughed when Ms. Baker brought her in a plate and sat it in front of her. The huff that accompanied it made them all laugh. It was Charlie who asked for her to tell them what they'd eaten in Welsh.

"Ah, but that's nothing more than pork chops, *golwythion porc. Tatws hufennog* was the creamed potatoes. Ms. Baker's son, he raises the goats we use for the cream. *Ffa gwyrdd*, of course, is the green beans. I think beans of some sort are had at every meal around here. I did think about serving you cawl, but I thought I'd wait a while for that treat." Charlie asked if she liked it. "No. I do not. The bread is laverbread. I don't care for that much either, but you guys seemed to like it. Would you like to know what's in it?"

As one they said no. Pete laughed as she finished off her dinner with a large glass of dark beer. Ms. Baker brought anyone that wanted one in too when they asked what she was drinking.

Booker was impressed with Pete. She wasn't comfortable by any means with them around her. She would stiffen up when someone got too close. However, not Uncle Hank. She was very comfortable around him, and Booker thought they all noticed that and approved.

They were getting ready to go and see Shawn when Uncle Hank's cell phone rang as they were getting into the car. He called for Pete to take it from him, and that was when he noticed she'd not been going with them.

"It's Shawn. He wanted to make sure she brought him the extra blanket for him, as well as herself. I don't think she was going to come." Booker told Uncle Hank it didn't appear she was happy now. "No, they make a nice couple, the two of them. He just lights up when she fusses at him. I've never seen anything like it. He'll upset her just to hear her cursing at him in Welsh. I'm sure she's not calling him nice names anyway."

Booker laughed. When Pete came out of the house, mumbling in what he assumed was Welsh, he laughed again. Right up until she pinned him with her eyes. She was scarer then Charlie was, he thought in that moment.

"You'll keep your opinions to yourself. Unless you want that wife of yours to be raising a fatherless son." He nodded, then realized what she'd said. "Men. You're all about as dense as a taith gerdded fircs." He didn't ask, but did look at Charlie. At her nod, he picked her up and swung her around, only to put her back on her feet and hold her gently. "There you go again, being a dense rock. She's not going to break, you moron. Hug her like you mean it."

He did. And he continued to take his turn in hugging her when everyone else took their turn. Christ, he was going to be a father. He was going to call his dad and tell him as soon as he had a moment. A baby. His baby, and he couldn't have been happier.

AWARD WINNING, BESTSELLING AUTHOR

Kathi Barton, a winner of the Pinnacle Book Achievement award as well as a best-selling author on Amazon and All Romance books, lives in Nashport, Ohio, with her husband, Paul. When not creating new worlds and romance, Kathi and her husband enjoy camping and going to auctions. She can also be seen at county fairs with her husband, who is an artist and potter.

Her muse, a cross between Jimmy Stewart and Hugh Jackman, brings her stories to life for her readers in a way that has them coming back time and again for more. Her favorite genre is paranormal romance, with a great deal of spice. You can visit Kathi on line and drop her an email if you'd like. She loves hearing from her fans. aaronskiss@gmail.com.

Follow Kathi on her blog: http://kathisbartonauthor.blogspot.com/